The HOUSE of SECRET TREASURE

KITA MITCHELL
Illustrated by Isabelle Follath

SCHOLASTIC

Published in the UK by Scholastic, 2021
Euston House, 24 Eversholt Street, London, NW1 1DB
Scholastic Ireland, 89E Lagan Road, Dublin Industrial Estate, Glasnevin,
Dublin, D11 HP5F

Text © Kita Mitchell, 2021
Illustration © Isabelle Follath, 2021

The right of Kita Mitchell and Isabelle Follath to be identified as the
author and illustrator of this work has been asserted by them under the
Copyright, Designs and Patents Act 1988.

ISBN 978 07023 0355 5

A CIP catalogue record for this book
is available from the British Library.

Printed by CPI Group (UK) Ltd, Croydon, CR0 4YY
Paper made from wood grown in sustainable forests
and other controlled sources.

This di

The HOUSE of SECRET TREASURE

For siblings everywhere

ONE

"Jess?"

My sister looked up from her porridge. "What?" she said.

"Did you finish off the jam?" I stared at her accusingly. "Because yesterday, there was loads left, and *now*, there isn't."

Jess shrugged. "I got back late from swimming," she said. "I made myself a sandwich."

"With a whole pot of jam?"

"I didn't eat *all* of it, George."

I peered into the empty jar. "Um . . . I think you *did*."

"Sorry." She didn't *look* sorry as she shovelled in her breakfast. "I was hungry."

"You should try and remember there are other people in this house," I said. "Who *also* like to eat."

"I said I was sorry. Have some porridge?" Jess pointed to the pan on the hob. "I made loads. There's chia seed in it."

"Thanks, but no." I huffed. "Seed is for birds. I'm not a bird, I'm an eleven-year-old boy."

"Suit yourself." Jess sat back down and carried on shovelling. "Did Mum get any crumpets in, do you know?"

I liked crumpets. "No," I said. "She definitely didn't."

Jess eats a *lot*. She says she has to, as she's training for the County Swim Championships. She goes to the pool about a million times a week. Well, maybe not *quite* a million, but almost.

She's very competitive.

She likes to win.

She usually does.

If she *doesn't*, she sulks. Once, when Alice West beat her by a millisecond, Jess slammed her bedroom door so hard it cracked the ceiling. Mum was cross about that and told Jess there was nothing good about being a bad loser. "Learn from George," she said. "He's *always* gracious in defeat."

Jess opened her door and bellowed, "GEORGE HAS HAD A LOT OF PRACTICE," then slammed it again.

Rude!

She did say sorry to me later, for being mean.

I accepted her apology, but only because it was accompanied by a Mars Bar – and also, we both knew she was right.

I've never won anything.

I've not even been close.

Not being last is about as much as I can hope for.

Take swimming. Everyone *expects* me to be good because of Jess – and I *do* have my 200-metre badge – but last time I went the lifeguard mistook my backstroke for drowning and threw me a woggle. It wouldn't have been so bad if he hadn't shouted, "DON'T WORRY, MATE, I'M ON MY WAY" so everyone looked and gave him a clap.

My running isn't any better. When I started at Hamfield High, Tommy said if we put our names down for cross-country, we'd get out of maths.

It seemed like a good idea at the time.

Then Mr Jones, the head of PE, saw me on the start line. He told everyone I was Jess's brother, and said with a SMITH on the team, we'd win by miles.

No one was more surprised than me when I came in

first – but Jack's mum was quick to point out I'd taken a wrong turn and missed half the course.

Hamfield High, who hadn't lost the cross-country in seventeen years, were disqualified. Mr Jones hasn't spoken to me since.

I think I disappointed him.

Unlike Jess, who never disappoints *anybody*.

She's good at everything.

Every other word in her school report is "outstanding".

Mine says things like, *George attends class and completes his homework. Well done, George!* Then they put a nice big tick in the "**AVERAGE**" box.

Mum says she doesn't have favourites and she's proud of us both, but she never talks about *me* to the neighbours. If anyone ever asks Mum what *I'm* good at, she shows them the thumb pot I made in year six.

Average.

I've only *ever* been average.

It must be cool to be best at something. Not best in the world, of course. Just better than Jess. I'd like Mrs Kowalski next door to hear about something I did and come over and say, "Oh my, Fiona. Isn't George incredible? YOU MUST BE SO PROUD."

And Mum would bask in my glory and say, "Yes, Mrs

Kowalski. George always *was* the one to watch." And Jess would simmer, green with envy, in the background.

I looked up at Jess's shelf full of trophies, then down at my un-jammy toast.

I was fed up with being average.

I was going to *do* something.

TWO

The question was, what?

I decided to start by ruling out all the stuff I wasn't good at – then I could see what was left.

Things I wasn't good at included ~~swimming, running, cricket, tenn~~... *all* sport, music – specifically the tuba, clarinet and violin – art, craft, ballet, tap, cooking, and anything to do with maths and spelling.

That didn't leave a lot.

I thought hard. I *quite* liked science – and I had a second-hand chemistry set upstairs. Perhaps I could invent something? A potion that cures boils, maybe? That would be excellent! *And* easy. The more I thought about it, the better it seemed. Oh my. A potion! I could win a Nobel Prize for that. They awarded those for all *sorts* of things. Woohoo! I bet the trophy would be enormous! Jess would have to move some of hers to make room for—

"George!"

Her screech cut through my deliberations.

I looked up. "What?"

Jess pointed at something small and brown trundling past the margarine tub.

It was an earwig.

Jess doesn't like earwigs. She doesn't much like dogs, cats, horses or cows either – but earwigs completely freak her out. She can't explain it. She thinks it might have something to do with their teeny-tiny pincers.

This one lives outside by the bins. He's always popping in and scampering around the table. His name's Harold.

"Don't just sit there," Jess squawked at me. "Get rid of it."

I took a bite of toast. "Usual terms?"

Jess nodded. "A pound."

I scooped Harold up. "Jess?"

"What?"

I pointed at her nose. "I notice you have a spot?"

"So?" She glared at me.

7

"Would you have any use for boil cream?"

Jess said some stuff that made me think she was quite anti the boil cream idea. Probably because she hadn't thought of it herself.

I took Harold out and watched as he disappeared under a log. I *loved* Harold. He was so cute. Maybe I could teach him some tricks?

I blinked.

Tricks.

That's what I could do! I couldn't believe I hadn't thought of it before. I'd work with animals. Become an animal trainer extraordinaire!

I hugged myself in excitement. I'd need a bit of practice, but when I got good, famous people would be queuing up for me to train their pets.

Trainer to the stars!

I could have my own YouTube channel!

I'd have a million followers and people would pay me to wear cool stuff, like hats and shades and puffer jackets.

Jess would be SO jealous.

Right. I'd need something to practise on. I could *start* with earwigs, of course – but a proper pet would be better. A dog? No. Anyone could train a dog. It couldn't be anything *regular*. I needed something with YouTube potential.

A llama?

Yes. A llama would be good.

I looked around our yard. Maybe not a llama. There was barely room for the bins.

A possum, then?

Possums were cute.

I'd wait for a good time, then ask Mum about a possum. If I told her it was a type of guinea pig, I bet she'd agree.

By the time I got back to my breakfast, Jess had found the crumpets and was on her third.

"Want one?" she asked.

I shook my head. I was too excited by my new idea to be interested in crumpets. I couldn't wai—

My thoughts were interrupted by the doorbell.

"I'll go." Jess jumped up. "I'm expecting some goggles. They're special ones," she explained. "Streamline."

Jess spends all her pocket money on stuff she thinks will make her swim faster. I'm sure none of it works. Once I borrowed her cone-shaped swim hat for a school gala, and I still came last. Also, I looked ridiculous.

She didn't come back with any goggles. She came

back with a letter. "It's not even for me," she huffed. "It's for Mum." She threw it on the table. "I had to sign for it."

Sign for it? I blinked. You only had to sign for things that were important, didn't you? It had better not be from school about my mock results. I'd done my best – but according to *some*, my best isn't good enough.

I peered across. The letter didn't *look* like it was from school. The envelope was thick and white and had a proper stamp on it. Across the top it said FIRST CLASS, then underneath that, PRIVATE. The flap had tape on it.

I held it up to the light.

"Tried that," Jess said. "I couldn't see anything. You'll have to wait until Mum gets home."

I put it down with a sigh. Mum wouldn't be back for ages. She's always working late. Her and Dad split up last summer and she says we need the money.

I looked at Jess. She was stuffing in the last crumpet. "If you ate less," I said, "Mum could go part-time."

"If I *ate* less," Jess said, "I wouldn't have a chance to be an Olympic champion and *therefore* would have no winnings to buy us a nice house." She paused. "George?"

"What?"

"You just knocked your orange juice on to that letter."

THREE

Jess put the letter on the radiator to dry, then forgot about it until teatime the following Sunday.

"Honestly, Jess." Mum wasn't very pleased. "It's been there nearly a week." She pulled the tape off the back and said she hoped that "whatever was inside" wasn't urgent.

"It doesn't *say* URGENT." Jess tried to get back into Mum's good books. "It says PRIVATE. If it had said URGENT, then I'm sure I wouldn't have forgotten."

"*Such* a silly place to put it," I mused.

"It's your fault." Jess glared at me. "If you hadn't tipped juice over it, I'd never have put it there."

"You can't blame *me*," I said. Jess wasn't often in trouble, so this was great.

"Oh, for goodness' sake." Mum scowled at us, then pulled a crumpled sheet from the envelope. "It's a good thing the ink hasn't run," she said.

She read down the page, then turned it over to check there was nothing on the back.

I waited for her to say something – but she didn't.

"Not from school, is it?" I asked, casually.

"No." Mum shook her head.

Phew. A weight lifted.

Jess looked over. "Who *is* it from, then?"

Mum paused. "A solicitor," she said. "A Mr Henry Wickom."

I blinked. A solicitor? Why would a *solicitor* be writing to Mum?

"Is everything OK?" Jess asked.

Mum put the letter down. "It's Mary Smallbone," she said.

I almost dropped my fork. Mary Smallbone? Miss Smallbone from the park?

I *loved* Miss Smallbone. I hadn't seen her for *ages*. "How is she?" I asked.

That turned out to be an uncomfortable question.

Miss Smallbone was dead.

"Dead?" I blinked at Mum.

She nodded. "I'm sorry, George. I know you really liked her."

"What did she die of?"

Mum peered at the letter again. "It doesn't say. She was quite old, I suppose. We've been invited to her memorial service."

"Oh," I said. I put my fork down. I didn't feel like eating any more. Poor Miss Smallbone.

Dead.

That was so sad.

I thought back to the first time we'd met her. I was seven and Jess was ten and we'd gone to the park with our scooters. It was freezing, so there was hardly anyone else there.

Miss Smallbone was standing on the top of the slide, brandishing a plastic cutlass at a seagull that had stolen her lunch. "You thieving blackheart," she screeched. "Bring that back."

The gull took no notice. That was a mistake.

Miss Smallbone pulled a spud gun from her britches and took aim.

Jess squeaked in horror. "Is that a—"

"Don't worry," I said. "It fires boiled potatoes. Tommy's got one."

Miss Smallbone hadn't boiled *her* potatoes. A solid-looking Maris Piper whizzed past the gull's head, followed by a Desiree. He dropped Miss Smallbone's sandwich in fright and flew off.

I ran over and picked it up.

Miss Smallbone leant over the rail and pointed her cutlass at me. "I think, young sir, you'll find that's mine."

"It fell in some mud." I held it out. "You probably shouldn't eat it."

"Rubbish." Miss Smallbone reached down for it.

"Dirt's good for your immunities." She crammed what was left of the sandwich into her mouth, then took a swig from a brown bottle labelled TEA. "How else do you think I got to be so old?"

She *was* old. Old and small and strange-looking. Alongside the britches, she was wearing a feathery hat and frilly shirt with floaty sleeves. It wasn't how most people dressed for the park, but when she explained she was descended from pirates, it made perfect sense.

She was there with her dog, Boris. He was napping under a bench.

Boris was a wolfhound.

I'd never met a wolfhound before. They're MASSIVE. When he uncurled himself, Jess almost had a heart attack and said she was going home. She said she didn't like normal dogs, let alone ones the size of horses.

Boris liked *her*, though.

He was very enthusiastic in his liking.

"He can tell you're not a dog person." Miss Smallbone helped her up. "He's trying to change your mind."

Jess wiped slobber from her eye. "He won't," she said. "I'll never like dogs. They have no manners, and they smell."

Miss Smallbone covered Boris's ears. "How horribly

15

rude! Don't listen to her, Boris."

"I'm not being *rude*," Jess said. "I'm being honest."

"You need to spend more time with him," Miss Smallbone said. "You'll be best friends before you know it."

"I'm not sure we *will*," Jess said.

Miss Smallbone always seemed to be around after that. She might have been about a hundred, but she was brilliant fun. She showed us how to swashbuckle, and what to do if you get caught smuggling (run very fast).

Then, last summer, they built forty-seven houses on the park, so we couldn't go there any more.

The last time I saw Miss Smallbone was in the Co-op. I'd gone to buy a sherbet Dip Dab and she was buying a pineapple. She was ever so pleased to see me. She said she was working on something really important, which was why she hadn't come to visit us – but soon, she'd be in touch with some amazing news.

She wouldn't be now.

Jess gave a sudden giggle. "Do you remember her awful hat? The one with the feathers? And she taught you all those words."

Mum's eyebrows shot into her hair. "Which words?"

"Nothing *rude*," I said. I kicked Jess under the table.

16

"Pirate words. Like *beslubbering* and *giglet*."

"You called Mr Coles a bilge rat," Jess said. "And got a detention."

"George!" Mum looked at me in horror.

"I didn't know he was behind me," I said. "He snuck up."

"That's not the point." Mum tutted. "Miss Smallbone should have known better."

"She was a pirate," I said. "If Miss Smallbone was French, you wouldn't have minded her teaching me French words."

"She was *descended* from pirates," Mum said. "I'm descended from Henry the Eighth, but it doesn't mean I chop people's heads off."

Whatever. There was no point arguing with Mum. She always had to have the last word. "Does the letter say what happened to Boris?" I asked. "Has he anywhere to go?"

"He's not coming here," Jess said.

"Miss Smallbone said dogs were good for people, especially if they were uptight." I gave her a pointed look.

"I'm not uptight," Jess huffed. "I didn't *mind* him. He was just so slobbery."

"There's no mention of Boris." Mum looked at the letter again. "I expect he's got a new owner."

I hoped it was someone nice.

FOUR

Just before the forty-seven houses were built, Miss Smallbone had invited us for tea.

Mum and me and Jess.

She wrote down the address and said she'd expect us on Sunday at four. When we got there, Mum said we must be on the wrong street because all the regular houses had numbers and Miss Smallbone couldn't possibly live in that big one at the end.

We walked up and looked anyway.

It turned out she did.

There, carved on the crumbly brick archway, was the name.

Hogweed Hall.

Boris appeared from behind Miss Smallbone and introduced himself to Mum.

"What an absolute charmer." Mum mopped her face.

"Isn't he?" Miss Smallbone ushered us through the doorway. "This is the hall." She sneezed. "Excuse the dust."

Wow.

I stared in awe. It wasn't anything like *our* hall. Our hall was full of boots and swim bags and stuff to go to charity shops.

Our whole flat could fit in here three times over.

"Look at that *staircase*." Mum's eyes almost popped out of her head. "The *carving* on it."

"The oak from a thousand plundered ships." Miss Smallbone struck a dramatic pose. "Brought here by my ancestors."

The staircase spiralled around us to the upper floors, where, instead of a regular ceiling, a great glass dome let in the light.

Miss Smallbone pointed up at it. "Might look fancy," she said. "But the devil to clean. Gulls aim for it, I swear."

"It's incredible," Mum said. "And the *floor*." She gazed at the tiles laid in intricate patterns. "It's beautiful, isn't it, George?"

I was too busy staring at the cabinets stuffed with old books and candlesticks and tiny ships in bottles to admire the floor. None of my friends had houses like this – not even Tommy, and his dad's an accountant.

"There's a lot of cobwebs," Jess whispered.

"There always are in old houses," I whispered back. "I hope you've brought some pound coins?"

"Shall we go to the kitchen?" Miss Smallbone said. "I'll make some tea. It's this way." She led us past the stairs and down a corridor at the back.

"Who's in the portraits?" Mum looked at the frames lining the walls.

"Relatives," Miss Smallbone said. "Cut-throats, one and all. I'll tell you about them over tea."

I stopped for a closer look. It must be amazing to be related to pirates. I only had one aunt, on Mum's side, and her name was Jane. She sang in a choir and taught the recorder.

No wonder I was ordinary.

None of Miss Smallbone's aunts were called Jane. Miss Smallbone's aunts were called things like Twelve-Toe Tina, Big Bess and Beryl Brushface. They all brandished weapons and scowled fearsomely.

Jess came up behind me. "Have you seen Poopdeck Percy?" She pointed to the opposite wall and giggled. "He's the spit of you."

I peered over. Percy *did* have hair that stuck out in all directions, but he also had a lot of warts and was missing an ear. "Funny you should say that." I said. I waved towards Beryl Brushface. "I saw her whiskers and *immediately* thought of yours."

"I do *not* have whiskers." Jess stepped on my foot.

"I do *not* have warts." I stepped on hers.

"Cake?" Miss Smallbone called. "I made them especially."

Miss Smallbone was *definitely* on her best behaviour. She hadn't said a single pirate word in front of Mum. She must be trying to make a good impression.

The kitchen wasn't as big as the hall, but it was still huge. It was lined with cupboards that didn't match and chests of drawers and workbenches – rather than everything fitted and the same. Another portrait hung above the stove, in a great gold frame. Jess read the plaque. "Sidney 'Squid-Hands' Smallbone." She shuddered. "Imagine having *him* staring at you every day."

Sidney had an enormous beard and was dressed in

pantaloons and a waistcoat. He stood on the dock like he meant business. One hand gripped a blunderbuss, the other a monster cutlass. Behind him was a ship, its name painted in gold along the prow.

The Windy Pig.

"George? This is the pantry." Miss Smallbone flung open a door to a small room lined with shelves. "It's where we keep the snacks." She bustled into it and picked up a plate of cakes.

I stared in awe. Imagine. A whole *room* for snacks.

"It's bigger than my bedroom," muttered Jess.

Mum was peering through the window behind the sink. "The garden looks amazing," she said. "I'd love to see it."

"Let me take you out." Miss Smallbone popped the cakes on the table. "Help yourself, children." She turned to Mum. "Do you like roses?"

"I *do*." Mum trotted happily after her.

I hoped they wouldn't be ages. I was desperate to look around the rest of the house. I'd have a cake while I was waiting. They had fluffy pink icing and strawberries on top and looked really nice. I chose one and took a bite. Mmmm. They were deliciou—

Eh?

I stared at the cake in my hand with watery eyes. Why was my mouth on fire?

"Are you OK, George?" Jess peered at me.

"Oh yes." I nodded. "I'm just moved by how tasty these are. You *must* have one." I pushed the plate in her direction.

"Thanks." Jess tucked in.

I watched eagerly. I wasn't disappointed. She stopped chewing and looked at me in horror. *"Chilli,"* she said. "There's *chilli* in them?"

"It must be a pirate recipe," I said. "What shall we do? We can't leave them. It'd be rude."

"Boris." Jess jumped up. "Here, boy."

Boris didn't seem to mind the chilli taste at all and had scoffed both by the time Miss Smallbone came back in. She stomped the mud off her boots and picked up the teapot. "Your mum's going to look around for a bit," she said. "She's particularly taken with my hibiscus."

"Delicious cakes," Jess said.

Miss Smallbone nodded. "I *do* love to bake. Have another?"

"I'm good, thanks." Jess held up her hand. "Training later. I don't want to sink."

"George?"

"I'd love one, but I'm absolutely stuffed," I lied. I pointed at the portrait to distract her from the crumbs around Boris's snout. "Miss Smallbone. Who's that?"

Miss Smallbone looked up and gave a snort. "That," she said, "is my great-great-grandfather."

"He's cool," I said.

"Cool?" Miss Smallbone slammed the teapot on to the table. "Cool?" She stamped her foot. "Sidney Smallbone was a beef-brained butt-wipe."

I blinked at her sudden fury.

"A coxcomb. A maggot. A worm-livered, good-for-nothing swine." Miss Smallbone was purple. She snatched a mug from the side and held it out. "Here you go. See if you can get him in the eye."

The mug had darts in.

"Not your favourite relative, then?" Jess asked politely.

"No." Miss Smallbone took a dart and hurled it with all her might. It struck Sidney's bejewelled turtle-shell codpiece with a thud. "Take that, you scab-faced spit-weasel."

I glanced out of the window. Luckily, Mum was admiring the azaleas and didn't look like she'd be in for a while.

I turned back to Miss Smallbone. "What did he *do*?" I asked.

"A terrible, *terrible* thing. I found his journals in the attic. I couldn't believe what I was reading." She closed her eyes as if to block the memory. "He'd recorded every gruesome detail."

"Every gruesome detail of *what*?" Jess asked.

Miss Smallbone shook her head. "I can't say. It's too awful."

"Please, Miss Smallbone?" I gave her my best beseeching look. I was *desperate* to know.

Miss Smallbone stood firm. "I'm sorry, George. I must shoulder the burden alone. If I told you, you'd never get over it."

"I'm sure I *would*," I said.

Without warning, Miss Smallbone whipped out her spud gun and blasted her great-great-grandfather in the chops. "It's a stain on the family name," she said. "Don't ask again."

I blinked. Whatever Sidney Smallbone had done, she was *really* upset about it.

"Cup of tea?" said Jess.

"Thank you, Jess, but I have my own." Miss Smallbone pulled her brown bottle from her britches and took a swig. "That's better. Shall I show you around while your mum's enjoying the garden? We'll start in the vaults."

It seemed that *vaults* was a fancy word for cellar, and to get to them we had to go down some narrow stairs at the back of the kitchen. Jess agreed to give me two pounds to go in front of her, so if there were any spiders, they'd drop on me first.

"I'd charge her more, George," Miss Smallbone called up. "There are some big beasts down here."

I paused.

"We shook on it." Jess gave me a shove. "Hurry up."

I didn't really like the vaults. They were dark and damp and spooky. The only light came from a tiny window which looked out over the drive. There was a crate underneath it, and Miss Smallbone said that was where she stood to spy on visitors, in case they were unwelcome ones.

I walked further in. A fireplace took up most of one wall and the rest were lined with trunks and old furniture. Somewhere, something was dripping. I lifted the lid of an iron-bound chest, but a moth flew out, so I shut it again.

Miss Smallbone pointed to a heap of barrels. "Rum,"

she said. "Great stuff. All pirates ever drink. Came from *The Windy Pig.*"

I remembered the painting. "Sidney's ship?" I asked.

"Mine now," Miss Smallbone said. "She's in storage. I'll get her out soon. I'm planning a trip."

I stared at her in envy. Imagine owning a ship you could use whenever you felt like it? How amazing would *that* be?

"That's the door to the garden." Miss Smallbone waved down a stone passage. "But we're going this way." She herded us over to the fireplace and tapped the mantelpiece. "Third stone in." She looked at me. "Remember that, George. Might be useful." She pushed it.

There was a grinding noise, and a panel in the chimney breast slid back.

"Wow." Jess's eyes almost popped out of her head. "Are those *stairs?*"

"They certainly are." Miss Smallbone stepped into the opening. "Follow me," she said.

I'd never been *anywhere* with a secret staircase. I was so excited I didn't care it was narrow and dark and dusty and there were scurrying noises and that Jess squawked about rats all the way to the top.

We tumbled out into the attics.

Miss Smallbone flung open a trunk. "Pirate clothes," she announced. She flung open another. "Trinkets." And another. "Maps."

We dressed up in flouncy shirts and eyepatches and played deck quoits with stuffed parrots – and when we were tired of that, Miss Smallbone showed us photos of when she was younger, riding her pony and learning to fly a plane.

I could have stayed up there for ever, but Miss Smallbone said she'd quickly show us the turret, and then we should make the most of Mum mooning over the roses and slide down the staircase on tea trays.

Mum wasn't too pleased when she came in.

"It's *four floors!*" she shrieked. "They're only little."

"Would you like a go?" Miss Smallbone landed in a heap in front of her.

Mum said no, thank you very much, she wouldn't. Then she said we had to go home.

"I'll show you the shrunken heads next time," Miss Smallbone called after us.

There never was a next time, and now there never would be.

FIVE

The letter said Miss Smallbone's memorial service was tomorrow.

I wanted to go. I'd really liked Miss Smallbone. Also, if some of her pirate relatives turned up, I could ask them about Sidney.

I still wondered about the terrible thing he'd done.

Jess said she was sorry, but she wasn't coming. Saying goodbye to dead people made her sad – and anyway, she couldn't at short notice. It was too close to the championships.

Mum said if Jess had given her the letter when she should have done, it wouldn't *be* short notice. She said we would *all* go. She'd take the day off work and it wouldn't hurt Jess to miss training for once.

It's great when Jess sulks. Peaceful.

Miss Smallbone's memorial was in a hall, next to where the park had been. We weren't the first to arrive. A man wearing a waistcoat and bright red trousers was arranging flowers in a vase.

Mum walked over. "Mr Wickom?"

The man swung around. "Ms Smith?" He grabbed Mum's hand and shook it. "Thrilled you could make it. Miss Smallbone would be so pleased."

"I only met her once or twice," Mum admitted. "She was good friends with the children. They were very fond of her."

"Mum thought she was bonkers," I said.

Mum stepped on my foot. "I didn't," she said.

"You must be George?" Mr Wickom beamed at me. "*So* pleased to meet you. Miss Smallbone told me you'd make an excellent coxswain." He gave me a hearty wallop across my shoulders.

"Did she?" I stepped away in case he did it again. I had no idea what a coxswain was. I'd google it before I took it as a compliment.

Mr Wickom waved at Jess, who'd stopped at a safe

distance. That was good. If Mr Wickom had given *her* a wallop, she'd have given him one right back.

"Are many others coming?" Mum asked.

"Mary's sisters," Mr Wickom said. "Mildred and Muriel."

I didn't know Miss Smallbone had sisters. She'd never mentioned them.

"Ah." Mr Wickom cocked his head. "Here they come."

The hall door crashed open and a tall woman in furs burst in, followed by a shorter one wearing a ballgown. They stood and looked around, in the manner of meercats. The one in the furs saw the clock and gave an annoyed tut. "We're late," she said. "A pox on you, Muriel. I *knew* we should have got a cab."

"They wouldn't start without us, Mildred dear." Muriel gave a giggle. "We're the important ones." She peered over at Mr Wickom. "Where would you like us to sit?"

He waved towards a

33

row of chairs. "Anywhere here."

"Have you organized snacks?" Muriel tottered over and sat down. She kicked off her shoes, which were high and shiny, and inspected her feet. "Bunions," she announced. "Such a curse."

"Did she think the invitation said 'party'?" Jess whispered.

"Looks like it," I whispered back. Muriel's voluminous skirts spilled out from under a velvet cape, and a large bow was perched on top of her carefully arranged curls.

Mildred plonked herself down next to her. She glanced at us, then turned back to her sister.

"Who are they?" she muttered.

"No idea," Muriel muttered back. "They can't be relatives. We haven't any left."

"Martin?" Mildred narrowed her eyes.

Muriel gave a snort. "Don't be ridiculous."

"They never found his body."

Muriel shook her head. "If Martin was alive ..." She rummaged in her bag and pulled out a doughnut. "... he'd be here now, staking his claim."

That sounded interesting. Who was Martin? Another relative? I should introduce myself, then, if I got the chance, I'd ask them about Sidney Smallbone and the terrible thing he did.

I sat down next to Mildred. "Hi," I said. "I'm George."

Mildred turned. She lifted a set of pince-nez and peered at me through them, but she didn't say anything.

I tried again. "I know Miss Smallbone from the park," I said.

Mildred leant across so her lips were inches from my ear. "I don't like children," she whispered. "Would you mind moving?"

Eh? I stared at her with my mouth open. How rude! I mean, *lots* of people don't like children, but they don't generally say so.

"He probably wants a doughnut." Muriel peered at me. "He's not getting one."

I didn't want a doughnut! I closed my mouth and glared at her and then I shuffled along so I was next to Jess. "What's wrong?" she asked.

"Nothing," I said. "Nothing at all." I glanced sideways at Miss Smallbone's sisters. No wonder she'd never mentioned them. They were horrible.

Mr Wickom cleared his throat. "We'll make a start, shall we? Mildred?" He turned to her. "Would you like to share any memories?"

Mildred shook her head. "I'm too upset." She dabbed her eye. "Poor dear Mary."

She didn't look upset to *me*.

Mr Wickom turned his gaze to Muriel. "How about—"

Muriel pulled out a large lace hanky. She blew her nose loudly, then mopped some jam from the bodice of her dress. "I couldn't," she said. "I'm also too upset." She took another large bite of her doughnut and munched loudly.

I stared at them. This was a strange sort of memorial. Why had they even bothered coming?

Mildred looked at her watch, then at Mr Wickom. "You did *bring* the will, didn't you?"

"Of course." Mr Wickom patted his jacket.

Muriel gave him an encouraging smile. "Read it, then. We're busy people."

"Of course, of course." Mr Wickom reached into his pocket and pulled out an official-looking piece of paper. "Here we have it. The last will and testament of Miss Mary Smallbone." He beamed around the room. "It's fairly straightforward."

"All we want to *know*," Mildred snapped, "is who gets Hogweed Hall?"

Mr Wickom ran his eye down the paper and then

turned it over. "That's an easy one," he said. "She's left it to George."

SIX

"Did Miss Smallbone just leave you her *house*?" Jess was staring at me.

She wasn't the only one.

Mildred was staring too, her mouth opening and closing like a fish.

Mum looked confused.

Muriel burst into tears. "Are you sure that's the right will?" Her voice came out as a strangled squawk. "Because the one that *we*—"

Mildred elbowed her sister hard. "What Muriel *means*," she said, quickly, "is that we were under the *impression*, as Mary's *only* relatives, that *we* would inherit?"

Mr Wickom shook his head. "There's no mistake.

Mary made her wishes perfectly clear." He slapped me on the back. "Congratulations, George."

Eh?

I owned a *house*?

And not just any old house.

Hogweed Hall.

Mildred looked like she was seething, but she managed a few words. "I'd have thought she'd want Hogweed to stay in the family, but clearly not. Well done, George. *Very* well done."

"Has she left him *everything*?" Mum sounded incredulous.

"Not *quite* everything," Mr Wickom said.

"No?" Muriel looked up eagerly.

"She left Jess something too."

Jess blinked. "What?"

"Boris."

Jess's mouth opened and shut almost as many times as Mildred's had. "I don't even *like* dogs," she said. "Miss Smallbone knew that. Why would she leave me *Boris*?"

Mr Wickom shrugged. "She didn't say."

Mildred muttered something into Muriel's ear.

Jess turned hopefully. "Did you want him?" she asked. "Because if you do, he's yours."

"Kind of you to offer." Mildred glared at her. "But no." She stood up. "Come on, Muriel. There's nothing for us here."

"On my way." Muriel jammed her feet back into her shoes and pulled on her cape.

"Bye," I said.

Mildred gave me a look.

It wasn't a nice look.

It was the sort of look that, if I hadn't already been with Mum and Jess and Mr Wickom, I'd have gone and found a grown-up to stand with.

I knew why she was cross.

They'd wanted Hogweed Hall, and Miss Smallbone had left it to me.

Mum saw they were leaving and got to her feet. "Mildred," she said. "I must have a word."

"It'll have to be quick." Mildred scowled and tapped her watch. "Luncheon, you know."

"This has been *extremely* unexpected," Mum said. "A shock, in fact."

"You're telling me," Muriel muttered.

Mum looked anxious. "You were expecting to inherit that house, and it's been left to someone you've never even met. I just wanted to check you were all right about it."

Mildred gave a tinkling laugh. "What a dear you are," she said. "There's no need for you to worry about *us*. We're over the moon for George."

Mum looked relieved. "Really?"

"Absolutely," Mildred said. "We have an enormous house of our own, and *wads* of cash. We'd have liked Hogweed Hall for *sentimental* reasons." She placed her hand on Mum's arm. "It was our family home, after all."

"Come to tea?" Mum said. "Perhaps you can choose a memento? Something to remember your sister by?"

"How *very* kind." Mildred's eyes lit up. "We would *love* to, wouldn't we, Muriel?"

Muriel gasped. "A visit to Hogweed? To choose a memento? We certainly *would*. Can we have anything we like?" She gave a little clap.

I stood there with my mouth open. What was Mum thinking? I didn't want Mildred and Muriel coming to my new house and taking my stuff! I was about to say so when Mum jammed her elbow into my ribs. "That's OK, *isn't* it, George?"

"Of course," I said, glaring at her.

"It'll be wonderful to see the old place again," Mildred said.

"Oh yes. It's been *years*." Muriel nodded earnestly.

"Years and years. Hasn't it, Mildred? The night Father died, in fact. Oh, there was a *terrible* row—"

My ears pricked up. This sounded interesting.

Mildred interrupted her. "We really *must* be off. It's been *charming* to meet you all." She gave us a smile that showed all her teeth. "We'll be round to visit just as soon as we hear you've moved in. Tootle pip."

She shoved Muriel towards the exit. "We need to make another plan," she muttered. "Pronto."

The door slammed behind them.

SEVEN

I'd inherited a house! And not just any old house.

Hogweed Hall!

It was going to be *amazing*.

I'd have Tommy over every weekend. We'd tea tray down the stairs and play sardines in the turret and—

Mr Wickom interrupted my thoughts to tell me about the *small print* of the will. "There's just a few conditions," he said. "Nothing to worry about."

Conditions are *rules*. I'm not fond of rules. "What are they?" I asked.

"Hogweed Hall is to be a home for all of you."

I stared at him. *That* was annoying. In my head I'd been living on my own.

Mum looked worried. "I hadn't thought we'd live there. We couldn't afford to run it."

I stared at her in horror. Not *live* there?

"No need to worry," Mr Wickom reassured her. "All bills are covered."

"Really?" Mum blinked. "For how long?"

"Fifty years."

"Fifty years?" Mum looked gobsmacked.

"You can give up work." Mr Wickom beamed.

"I'm not giving up work." Mum looked affronted. "I like my job."

"Can I interrupt?" Jess asked. "I don't have to *accept* Boris, do I?"

"I'm afraid you do," Mr Wickom said. "Miss Smallbone wanted him to stay at Hogweed."

Jess looked at me. "I could sell him to you?" she said.

I wasn't sure. We'd have space for a llama now. Two pets might be hard work. "I'll think about it," I said.

"There's one last thing." Mr Wickom busied himself with some papers. "The tenants."

"The what?" Mum stopped dead.

"The tenants. Miss Smallbone rented out part of the house. Nothing to worry about. They won't get in your way."

"Oh." Mum looked nervous. "Who did she rent it to, exactly?"

Mum assumes everyone she doesn't know is an axe murderer. I don't know why. There are never any axe murder stories in the *Hamfield Gazette* – and you'd think there would be if there were so many around.

"There's Marta," Mr Wickom said. "She lives in the basement. She's Polish. A pastry chef. Agoraphobic. You'll hardly ever see her."

Mum relaxed a little. An agoraphobic pastry chef couldn't be too bad. "Who else?"

"Dr Gupta. She has a lab in the attic."

"A doctor?" Mum's expression switched from nervous to impressed.

"A geneticist," Mr Wickom said. "She worked at the National History Museum until last year." He looked at his watch. "We could walk over and meet them now, if you like?"

"I'd love to," I said.

Really, I just wanted to see my house.

"George?" Jess caught up with me. "Have you thought any more about Boris?"

I looked at her. "How much do you want for him?"

"Three hundred pounds."

I blinked. Was she kidding?

"I can't sell him for less," Jess said. "I need a new race suit for the county championships."

"That's a lot for a swimming costume," I said.

"They're made of special material," Jess explained. "Olympians wear them. They squash you in and make you swim faster."

"You always win anyway," I said.

"I'd win *better*," Jess said. "What do you think?"

"I've only got nine pound fifty," I said. "Sorry."

Jess sighed. "Forget the race suit. Nine pound fifty and he's yours."

I shook my head.

She glared at me. "OK. You can *have* him."

I like free stuff – and I did like Boris – but I really wanted a llama.

"I'll take him for walks sometimes," I said. "If you pay me."

"Here we are." Mr Wickom stopped at the gate. "All yours. How are you feeling, George?"

"Brilliant," I said.

Who wouldn't?

I gazed up at the turret on my house.

Miss Smallbone had called the turret the crow's nest.

46

When we went for tea that time, she'd had taken us to the platform at the top and let us have a go with her spyglass. She told us to look for marauders and got her spud gun ready, just in case.

There hadn't been any marauders that day, which was a shame. You could see for *miles* though. It'd been brilliant.

And now it was mine.

Mum gawped up at it. "I'd forgotten how lovely it was," she said. "When did Miss Smallbone say it was built?"

"I'm not sure she did," I said.

"That could be a date." Jess pointed up above the porch. "Carved into that stone? I think it's Roman numerals."

I squinted up. "I can see an M," I said. "The rest of it is missing."

"Maybe it was struck by lightning?" Jess said.

I wasn't really interested in how the stone got damaged. I wanted to go inside. I ran up the steps after Mr Wickom. He unlocked the door and gave a little bow. "After you, George."

"Thank you," I said. I stood there for a moment.

A house built by pirates.

Lived in by pirates.

Not any more, though. From now on it was lived in by *me*.

I took a breath and stepped into the hall.

Oh *my*.

It was bigger than I remembered. I sneezed. And dustier.

Nothing had changed. The chandeliers still glimmered under their coating of dust, portraits still lined the walls – and there, ahead of me, loomed the great staircase.

A cobweb floated above my head.

"It's so *quiet*," I said.

It wasn't for long. A thunderous bark came from below.

"That'll be Boris. Marta's been looking after him for you, Jess," Mr Wickom said.

"Any chance she'd like to keep him?" Jess muttered.

EIGHT

Miss Smallbone had converted part of the cellar into a flat. The kegs had been moved and the walls were white and there were lights and proper tiles on the floor and not as many dripping pipes.

There was a note taped to Marta's door.

Had to pop out on emergency business. Let yourself in and have a biscuit.

Marta

PS Boris's poo bags are on side. He'll probably need to go.

I tried the door.

Oh.

One minute I was staring into a dark hallway and the next I was knocked flying by a great heap of fur and slobber. Boris was even *more* pleased to see Jess. She pushed him off and got up. "I'm covered in saliva," she complained. "It's disgusting."

Honestly. She wasn't even *trying* to bond with him. I handed her the roll of bags and a shovel. "Marta says could you take him out?"

She stomped off down the passage. "I'm supposed to be training," she shouted. "You'll be sorry when I lose."

Boris bounded after her. I was going to follow but suddenly remembered Marta's note had mentioned biscuits? I'd just go in and grab one.

There wasn't much in Marta's living room, just the fireplace at one end and an armchair next to it. The only window was the one that looked out on to the drive. It was more overgrown with weeds than ever.

Ah. There were the biscuits. A plateful of home-made biscuits on the side. They looked delicious! Two buttery slabs sandwiched together with vanilla filling. I took the biggest and bit into it.

Eh?

Curry?

They tasted of curry.

Don't get me wrong. I *like* curry. IN *CURRY*!

I thought back to the chilli

50

cupcakes. Marta must be using Miss Smallbone's pirate cook book.

"They look nice." Mum had come in with Mr Wickom.

I swallowed. "Unusual," I croaked. "I'm not sure you'd like them."

"Polish spices, maybe?" Mr Wickom said.

Jess stomped back in. "Ooh, biscuits," she said.

"Take two, why don't you." I offered her the plate.

"We've got time to say hello to Dr Gupta," Mr Wickom said. "I'm afraid your lovely doggy isn't allowed in the lab. You'll have to leave him down here."

"He can have the rest of my biscuit," I said.

"And mine." Jess glared at me. "I mean they are *delicious*, but a bit too rich."

"What's Dr Gupta working on?" Mum asked as we headed up the stairs.

"It's a secret," Mr Wickom said. "I did ask, of course, but she wouldn't say."

A secret? I *loved* secrets. I'd make friends with Dr Gupta and then she'd tell me.

"This way." Mr Wickom swerved across the third-floor landing and up a second staircase. This one wasn't carved from the oak of a thousand plundered ships. It was plain and narrow and went straight up until it suddenly turned left and out on to a corridor. "Down here." Mr Wickom trotted ahead. He stopped at a door and pressed a bell. No one came, so he pressed it again.

This time we heard quick footsteps, followed by the rattle of a chain. The door flew open with a bang. "Yes?"

The woman standing in front of us wore a white coat and a fearsome scowl. She was holding a sandwich. Egg, if I wasn't mistaken. I took a step back. If this was Dr Gupta, she didn't look like she'd be sharing her secrets with me any time soon.

Mr Wickom gave a nervous squeak. "Terribly sorry to interrupt. I've popped up to introduce Fiona, Jess and . . ." He shoved me forward. "George."

Dr Gupta stared at me.

There was an uncomfortable silence.

"How do you do?" I held out my hand.

Dr Gupta ignored it. She scowled at Mr Wickom over my head. "She went through with it, then?"

Mr Wickom shuffled nervously. "Yes," he said. "She did."

"Went through with *what*?" Jess asked.

"You mean leaving everything to George?" Mum stepped forward. "Yes. We were surprised too."

Dr Gupta snorted. "Such a *ridiculous* idea."

"Oh." Mum looked taken aback.

Mr Wickom changed the subject. "I explained you were a geneticist," he said. "I'm sure Jess and George would love to hear about your work?"

"I'm busy." Dr Gupta took a large bite of her sandwich. "I'm always busy."

Rude!

Mr Wickom reached inside his pocket. "I need to fill you in on—"

Dr Gupta interrupted him. "Mary's will?"

"That's right." Mr Wickom produced it with a flourish.

"She told me all about it." Dr Gupta picked a piece of cress from between her teeth.

"I wasn't sure if you knew the detail," Mr Wickom admitted.

"I do. The attics are mine to work in as long as I wish?"

"Yes," Mr Wickom, "that's right—"

"I shall be using the fire escape as my entrance so as to least disrupt George and his family?"

"Yes—"

"And Mary left me a sum of money to continue with this project in her absence?"

"Absolutely right." Mr Wickom beamed.

"Anything else?" Dr Gupta raised her eyebrows.

"I think that's it." Mr Wickom pushed the will back

into his pocket.

"Wonderful. Goodbye." Dr Gupta slammed the door in our faces.

"Gracious." Mum blinked. "She doesn't seem too pleased about the will either."

"Perhaps you could *not* offer her a memento?" I suggested. "I'd quite like some stuff left."

"While we're up here." Mr Wickom trotted off down the corridor. "I'll show you one more thing."

Jess followed him. "Did Miss Smallbone *know* she was going to die?" she said. "She was very organized, sorting out her will and telling people."

"We're all going to die." Mr Wickom sighed. "All of us. Best to be prepared."

"Sensible." Mum nodded.

I was just about to ask if anyone else had been annoyed by Miss Smallbone leaving me the house when I heard a noise.

A click.

I turned around to look.

The door to the lab had swung open. Just a tiny bit.

Dr Gupta's eye was glinting through the gap.

She was watching us.

I don't know why that made me nervous, but it did.

NINE

Mr Wickom turned down another corridor. This one was narrow and dark, with a door at the end. "Here we go." He gave the handle a tug, then another. "Strange." He looked confused. "It's a fire exit. It's not supposed to be locked." He tugged at it again.

"Push?" suggested Jess.

"Oh yes." Mr Wickom giggled. "Silly me."

Light flooded in.

A balcony!

"Oh my." Mum stepped forward. "Look at that!"

I followed her out. You could see the whole city! It was almost as good as the view from the crow's nest!

Mr Wickom pointed to some steps that zigzagged down to the garden. "Dr Gupta will come in and out this way. You'll barely see her."

"Is it always left unlocked?" Mum asked, brightly.

She was thinking about axe murderers again. I could tell.

"You can't open it from outside unless it's on the latch." Mr Wickom demonstrated. "I'll remind Dr Gupta to keep it shut."

Mum relaxed. She leant over the railing and looked down at the garden. "Oooh, look." She gave a little clap. "Chickens. They weren't there before."

"A recent venture." Mr Wickom's comb-over lifted in the breeze. "You'll have lots of eggs."

"I've *always* wanted chickens," Mum said.

"Plenty of room for a llama," I said.

Mum and Mr Wickom went down to the garden while Jess and I stayed up on the balcony.

"That's where the park used to be." Jess pointed. "And there's school."

Things looked completely different from above. I had a really good view of Mr Wickom's shiny bald spot, and... I leant over further. "What are those holes?" I pointed them out to Jess. "All over the lawn. There's loads of them."

Jess peered over too. "Molehills?"

I shook my head. "There's a spade. Someone's been digging."

"Digging for what?"

I turned to face her. "Treasure?"

"*Treasure?*"

"They were *pirates*," I reminded her. "I bet the garden's full of it. Maybe Miss Smallbone was digging stuff up before she died?"

Jess peered down. "Do you think there's any left? If I found some, I could afford my race suit."

"If you find any," I said, "we have to split it. It's only fair, as it's my house."

"OK." Jess shrugged.

I suddenly felt bad. If *Jess* had been left a huge house with treasure in the garden, and I hadn't, I'd have been furious.

"Don't you *mind*?" I asked.

"Mind what?"

"Miss Smallbone leaving her house to me?"

"No." Jess turned to face me. "I get to live here too. It's great."

"Because," I went on, "if you *did mind*, you shouldn't."

Jess frowned. "What do you mean?"

"All the good stuff happens to you."

"No, it *doesn't*." She glared at me.

"It does." I glared back. You're always winning things."

"Only swimming galas," Jess said. "They're hardly exciting."

"Mum thinks they are. She's never stops talking about you. She never talks about *me* to anyone. It's not very nice listening to her go on and on and on, knowing you're her favourite."

Jess looked outraged. "I'm *not* her favourite!"

"You *are*," I said.

"I can see why you might think that," Jess agreed. "But she's always showing people your thumb pots."

"It's not the same," I said. "You're good at everything, and I'm not."

Jess scowled. "It's not always *fun*, you know, being good at stuff."

"You're just saying that."

She shook her head. "People have *expectations*. I have to work really hard so I don't let them down." She picked a bit of flaky paint off the rail. "Sometimes it's OK, but

58

most of the time it's boring."

"It does *look* boring," I agreed. "Swimming up and down for hours on end."

"Mum's always going on about me getting to the Olympics. Suppose I don't?" Jess looked at me. "She'll be really disappointed."

"I guess."

"Sometimes, on my way to galas, I feel like getting a bus in the opposite direction."

"To where?" I said.

"Anywhere." Jess headed down the steps. "Anywhere but the pool."

I stared after her.

I thought Jess loved being a champion.

Maybe being good at everything was harder than I realized?

At least people only expected me to do my best, not win the Olympics.

Mum had got as far as the bedrooms by the time we caught up with her. She was raving about one covered in floral wallpaper with a hideous feathery lampshade hanging over the bed. "Just look, Jess," she said. "It's gorgeous. *Gorgeous.*" She paused. "Would anyone mind if I had this room? Though of course I won't if either of you want it?"

"It's not really my style," I said, politely.

Jess said she didn't mind which bedroom she had. In the end, she decided on a blue one overlooking the garden. "I'll have to have a clear-out though," she said. "The wardrobe's rammed full of junk."

"Don't throw out anything important," I said.

Jess rolled her eyes. "I won't," she said.

I already knew which room I was going to have. The one in the turret. It had stairs that led to the crow's nest. I couldn't think of a better place to sleep.

TEN

It didn't take long to pack everything. Mum hired a van and left the landlord a rude note about damp patches – and we were off.

Even though it was raining, Boris was waiting for us on the steps. He was very pleased to see Jess – much more pleased than Jess was to see him, at any rate. She ranted that wet dog was actually a thousand times worse than dry dog, then muttered something about eBay.

The lights were on in the attic. Dr Gupta must be home. Marta wasn't, though. She'd left us a note on the kitchen table:

Welcome to Hogweed Hall! I was called away to see a sick aunt but I've made you some muffins. Help yourself.

I didn't mind if I did! I pulled the lid off a tin next to

the note. Oooh. Choc chip! With swirly fudge icing and Smarties! *Delicious.* I reached in and took one.

Then, just before I took a bite, I stopped. I stopped because I remembered the biscuits Marta had left for us in her flat.

I gave the muffin a cautious sniff.

It *smelt* all right.

It didn't smell like curry.

It smelt good.

I took a big bite.

Mmmm— Oh.

Blurggh.

Gravy.

I was about to offer one to Jess when Mum came in with a pile of boxes. "Honestly," she said. "Some people." She didn't look very pleased.

"What's wrong?" I said.

"Mr Wickom just called," she said. "Mildred and Muriel are visiting this afternoon."

This afternoon? I stared at her in horror. We'd only just moved in! I had stuff to do! I didn't want Mildred and Muriel poking their noses everywhere!

"Sorry," Mum said. "I'd try and put them off, but I haven't got a number for either of them."

"We could hide?" I suggested. "And not answer the door?"

"The van's in the drive," Mum said. "And Boris will bark. Though we'll have to put him downstairs – Muriel's scared of dogs." She opened the door to the pantry. There wasn't much in it, just some half-empty jars of jam and a box of rat poison. "I have no idea where I packed the biscuits. We've got nothing to offer them."

"What's wrong with the rat poison?" I muttered.

Mum looked over. "Sorry, dear?"

"I said there's *muffins*." I waved at the tin. Mildred and Muriel were welcome to the gravy buns.

"That's something," Mum said. "But there's no milk for tea."

"Do you want me to see if Marta's got any?" I asked. "She might have some in her fridge?"

"Good idea." Mum emptied a box of cutlery into a drawer. "But if she hasn't, you'll have to go to the shop. There's one at the end of the street."

I blinked. It was pouring outside. How come *I* had to go to the shop? I wanted to arrange my bedroom! If it wasn't for *me*, we wouldn't even be living here. You'd think I'd be treated like I was a *little* bit special. It

was hardly *my* fault Mildred and Muriel were visiting!
"Can't Jess go?" I said.

"I'm busy," Jess said.

She clearly *wasn't*. "I shouldn't go on my own," I said.
"I'm only eleven. I might get kidnapped."

"Ha." Jess's eyebrows shot up. "Who'd kidnap you?"

"Jess has to get her things ready for training," Mum
said. "Try Marta first – if she's back it'd be nice to say hello."

I stomped downstairs. It wasn't fair. Jess always got
out of things because she swam. I should have been an
only child. If I was, I wouldn't be *compared* all the time –
and *I'd* be the favourite. I stopped and hammered on
Marta's door.

There was no reply. She must still be at her aunt's.

I really couldn't be bothered to go to the shop, so I
banged again, just in case she *was* in and hadn't heard
the first time.

This time there *was* a noise. Shuffling, followed by a
creak.

Then silence.

How strange.

I tried the handle. It wasn't locked, so I pushed it open.

"Hello?" I called. No one replied, so I walked to the
end of the hall and looked into the living room.

There was a colourful shawl draped over the armchair, but apart from that there was no sign anyone lived here at all.

If there was a noise, I must have imagined it.

I checked the fridge, but Marta didn't have any milk either. Just a pineapple.

The shop was at the end of the street. There was a noticeboard outside, so I went over to see if anyone local was advertising a llama. A large man with an enormous moustache was pinning up a poster. It seemed there was a dodo exhibition at the Natural History Museum. I liked dodos.

The man brushed a speck off his shiny beige suit. "Interested?"

I looked at him. "Are the dodos alive or dead?"

The man didn't realize I was joking. He blinked. "Dead, sonny. Dead as doornails. Or in this case, dodos. They're extinct."

I stared at him, coldly. "Are they?"

He pulled a sorrowful face. "Sorry to be the one to break it to you. You should come to the exhibition. You might learn something."

"Might I?"

"Tell you what." The man pulled a card from his inside pocket and wrote something on the back. He handed it to me. "Give them that at the door. They'll let you in. I'm Mr Mason. The curator."

I watched him walk away.

Mr Mason. How *rude* could someone be?

Did I *look* like someone who didn't know dodos were extinct?

I knew *loads* about dodos. No, I would *not* be going to his rubbish show.

I tore up the card and went in to get the milk.

ELEVEN

I took the milk to the counter and introduced myself to the man behind the till. "I expect you'll be seeing a lot of me," I said. "I've just moved in to Hogweed Hall." I didn't tell him Hogweed Hall was mine, in case he thought I was rich and overcharged me.

"Hogweed Hall?" The man looked interested as he scanned the milk. "The one at the end of the street with the turret? Built by pirates?"

"Yes," I said.

He handed me my change along with a flyer for the local dramatic society. "Seen the ghosts yet?" he said.

"Ghosts?" I blinked at him.

He held up his hand. "Sorry, mate. You're only little. I shouldn't have said anything."

Little? I stared at him in fury. I wasn't *little*. Little implied I was *young*. Short, yes, but not *little*. "I don't mind ghosts." I said, icily.

The man looked dubious. "You sure?"

I glared at him. "Yep."

"Well then." He leant closer. "The place is full of restless souls. There's been *murders* up there."

I stared at him. "Who was murdered?"

"I'm getting to that." He scowled at me.

"Sorry," I said.

"That house belonged to an old pirate, Scurvy Legs Smallbone. He'd had enough of cavorting around on high seas. His four children were born there. Martin, Mildred, Muriel and Mary."

Martin? My mouth fell open. Miss Smallbone had a brother? *That's* who Mildred and Muriel were talking about at the memorial!

The man went on. "Scurvy Legs was proud of his offspring. He cemented a stone above the door with four *M*s carved into it."

"Their initials?"

"That's right. Nothing was too good for them. Posh frocks and afternoon tea all the way. Their pirate days were well and truly behind them. Then ..." The man lowered his voice dramatically. "One dark night, Martin disappeared. Was never seen again."

I stared at him. "Murdered?"

The man shook his head. "Ran away to sea. His father was furious. The very next morning he climbed up and chiselled an M off that stone." He stopped. "This is where it gets gory. Maybe I—"

"It's fine," I said. "Go on."

The man seemed happy to. "Twenty years later, Scurvy Legs died of the pox. A tremendous storm raged outside that night – but even the thunder couldn't drown the screams coming from that house."

I gripped the milk.

"By morning, two of the sisters were gone."

"Gone?"

His voice dropped even further. "It's said," he whispered, "that the youngest sister murdered her siblings so she could inherit the house. After she buried their dismembered corpses in the garden, she climbed up with that chisel and chipped away two more of the Ms."

I blinked.

"The dead sisters still haunt the place. Saw one of the them the other day. Shot out the gates in the flouncy dress she died in. Covered in blood, it was."

69

"It's a very good story," I said. "And I don't want to spoil it, but Mildred and Muriel aren't dead."

The man looked annoyed. "How do you know?"

"They're coming for tea this afternoon." I picked up the milk and headed for the door.

As I walked back up the street, I thought about Miss Smallbone's brother.

Martin.

What happened to him?

I had a *lot* to ask Mildred and Muriel about.

TWELVE

By the time I arrived back with the milk, Mum had moved some of the boxes and put Marta's cakes on a plate.

I went to answer the bell when it rang. Hopefully they wouldn't take too long to choose a memento. I'd already spotted some hideous vases I'd be happy to let them have.

"George." Muriel had dressed for the occasion in a sparkly frock and feather boa. She tottered across the step. "How wonderful to see you."

Mildred could hardly be seen behind an absolutely massive bunch of flowers. "Where's your mother?" she asked.

71

"In the kitchen." I led the way.

Mildred and Muriel followed me, stopping every two seconds to admire something.

"It's so *long* since we've been in here," Muriel twittered. "It hasn't changed." She ran her finger along the side. "Maybe a little dustier?"

Mildred stopped by one of the portraits and smiled up at it. "Beryl Brushface. My dear aunt. She used to visit every Christmas. Always brought the pudding."

This might be a good time to ask.

"Do you remember anything about your great-grandfather?" I asked. "Sidney Smallbone?"

"Squid-Hands?" Mildred looked surprised. "What do you want to know?"

"I heard he'd done something terrible. Do you know what it was?"

Mildred blinked. "He was a *pirate*, dear. I expect there were lots of things."

"There wasn't anything *more* awful than all the other awful things?"

"Nothing that springs to mind," Mildred said. "Muriel? Can you think of anything?"

Muriel put her head on one side and thought for a while. "No," she said.

72

Well, *that* was disappointing.

Mum had found a tray to put a teapot and some china cups on, though none of them matched. "So glad you could come," she lied. "How are you both?"

"All the better for seeing you." Muriel thrust the bouquet into Mum's arms.

"Oh." Mum looked surprised. "Thank you."

"And chocolates." Mildred rummaged in her bag and pulled out an enormous box.

"Gracious." Mum blushed. "What a treat."

"It's the least we could do." Mildred beamed. "It was so kind of you to have us round."

"No trouble at all." Mum went even redder. "It's lovely to see you."

"You must be very busy." Muriel plonked herself down at the table. "But we just couldn't wait to come and see our old home. It's been *so* long."

"Why *has* it been so long?" Jess asked. "Did you and Mary fall out?"

"Oh yes—" Muriel began.

Mildred stuck her elbow in Muriel's ribs. "Not as such. There was friction after Father died. We let things drift."

73

Muriel looked solemn. "They always say you can't choose your family."

I eyed Jess. "I know *exactly* what you mean," I said.

"Tea?" Mum busied herself with the teapot.

"Please." Mildred gave her a toothy smile.

"Look at those muffins." Muriel clapped her hands. "Did you make them for us, darling George?"

Darling George? I blinked. They'd changed their tune. I shook my head. "Marta made them."

"Marta?" Mildred raised her eyebrows.

"She rents a flat in the basement," I said.

Muriel gasped. "Poor dear Mary. Renting out rooms? She must have been penniless."

"It does sound like it." Mildred seemed strangely pleased. "Why else would you take in lodgers?" She picked up the tray of cups. "Shall we go through to the parlour? Bring the cakes, Muriel." She bustled off.

Parlour? Where was the parlour?

The parlour was the big living room at the front. I'd only been in there once. The chairs were really uncomfortable and everything was red.

The wall at the back was mainly taken up with a portrait of *Twelve-Toe Tina, 1660–1682*.

Mildred stopped in front of it.

"Let me pour the tea." Mum took the tray from her. "Is she one of your relatives?"

"Our great-great-grandmother," Mildred said. "She was married to Sidney."

Muriel trotted over to join her. "A *dear* woman."

They both stood and stared at the painting.

"Tragic," Muriel murmured.

"What was?" Jess asked.

"She died young. Tropical fever," Mildred said.

"Sores all over," Muriel said. "Temperature of one hundred and eight. Her brain practically exploded."

"Gracious." Mum looked shocked. "How awful."

"It was." Muriel dabbed her eye. "It struck swiftly. Such a terrible shame. She choked on her tongue before she could reveal the hiding place of the Constantine Ruby."

"The what?" I said.

Mildred placed her hand on Muriel's arm. "I'm *sure* George doesn't want to hear our boring family history," she murmured.

"I *do*," I said. "Go on, Muriel."

Muriel shook off Mildred's hand and pointed to a ring sparkling on her great-great-grandmother's finger. "The Constantine Ruby. It's priceless. Sidney acquired it in a skirmish at the opera house. He gave it to his bride on their wedding day."

Mum gasped. "How romantic."

"Wasn't it," Muriel agreed. "It went missing years ago. *Years*. Father said that whoever tracked it down could keep it." She looked at Mildred. "We used to wonder if Mary had found it and kept it for herself, didn't we?"

"Sort of thing she'd do," Mildred muttered.

"She can't have, though." Muriel gave a giggle. "Because if she had, she'd be the richest woman in Europe – and she *clearly* isn't." She turned to Jess. "And you know what *that* means?"

"What?" Jess asked politely.

"It means the Constantine Ruby is still up for grabs!" She gave a little clap. "Finders keepers, Father said."

Mildred gave her a push. "Do stop prattling, Muriel. The children aren't interested."

Jess clearly was. "Have you any idea where the ruby might be?" she asked.

"No, none at all." Mildred sat down and reached for the teapot.

"We have our suspicions—" Muriel began.

"No, we don't," Mildred said.

"We *do*, Mildred." Muriel gave a tinkling laugh. "We were talking about it just the other day, remember?"

"I am sure we were *not*," Mildred snapped.

"You're getting old," Muriel tittered. She turned back to Jess. "We don't know for *certain*," she said, "but Mildred and I think it was buried on Hornswagg. Pirates *always* hid their most valuable pieces below ground."

I sat up straight. "Where's Hornswagg?" I asked. "Is it far?"

"It's an island," Muriel said. "Hornswagg Rock, to be precise. Sidney won it in an arm wrestle. From John the Pox. It's in the middle of the Indian Ocean."

"Do drink your tea, Muriel." Mildred glared at her. "You must be thirsty, all that talking."

Jess went over to take a closer look at the portrait. "What makes you think it's buried there?" she asked. "And not, say, in the garden *here*, at Hogweed?"

"*Because.*" Muriel pointed at the jewel sparkling on Tina's finger. "She was wearing the ring in *this* portrait, which was painted days before they set off on their honeymoon to Hornswagg—" She took a dramatic breath.

We waited.

"—and she's *not* wearing it in the one upstairs which was completed on their return." Muriel looked around triumphantly. "And then she died. Sidney never went back to Hornswagg after that."

She trotted over and sat down next to Mildred.

"Such a lovely tale, Muriel." Mildred looked sour. "We all enjoyed it. Thank you for sharing."

"Did you ever go to Hornswagg?" I asked. "To look?"

"No," Mildred snapped. "We didn't."

"The map to the island was lost," Muriel said. "Sidney put it in a safe place and forgot where, the lard-brained old foo— OW." She jumped up.

"Oops. *Silly* me." Mildred had spilled her tea in

Muriel's lap. She passed her a napkin. "Mop it up with that, dear. Now. I think we've heard enough about that old ruby," she said. "*Lovely* weather we're having for March."

"Isn't it," Mum agreed. "Who'd like a muffin?"

"Ooh, thank you." Muriel forgot about her damp skirt and took the largest. She crammed the whole thing in at once.

Hahaha. Gravy buns. I waited for her to spit it out.

She didn't.

She reached for another. "Delicious," she declared. "Just like Mary used to make."

Mildred bit into hers and nodded in agreement. "She must have given Marta the recipe."

I peered at the remaining muffins. Perhaps I'd been mistaken. After all, they did *look* nice.

"George? Do you want one?" Mum held out the plate.

"Thanks." I'd give them another go.

Blurggggh.

I *hadn't* been mistaken.

Gravy.

THIRTEEN

Mum started to clear up the tea things. She asked Mildred and Muriel if they'd decided on a memento. "I don't mean to be rude," she said. "But we have a lot of unpacking to do."

"There are some *lovely* vases," I hinted.

"Would you mind," Mildred said, "if we had a little longer to make up our minds? We'd like something that really held the *essence* of Mary."

"Of course," Mum said. "Take as long as you need. I'll have to get on though – I need to find the toothbrushes."

Mildred stood up. "We could have a quick look now, then drop in again at the weekend?"

"Oh." Mum flushed. "Actually, the weekend might

be tricky. I'm supposed to be going away with work tomorrow."

"Are you?" Jess looked surprised.

"I didn't want to say anything until I was sure," Mum said. "I got that promotion. They're sending me on a training course."

"That's brilliant." Jess gave her a hug. "Well done, Mum."

Mum winced. "It's for ten days. I'm sorry, Jess, I'll miss the swimming championships."

"I don't mind that," Jess said. "You've been to loads."

Ten days? No apology for me, I noticed! I folded my arms. "It's the Easter holidays," I said. "You can't go away. I'm supposed to be doing all sorts of things. Tommy was going to come over. He still doesn't believe I inherited a house."

"I know it's bad timing," Mum said. "I'll make it up to you."

Yeah, right. She *always* says that and then comes home with a bar of Dairy Milk. I scowled at her. "Who's coming to look after us?"

"Mrs Kowalski."

Jess froze. "Oh," she said. Then she said it again. "Oh."

"Jess?" Mum stared at her.

"I forgot to tell you."

"Tell me *what*?"

"Mrs Kowalski phoned yesterday. She said she had flu. She said she was really sorry, but she'd have to let you down."

"Jess!" Mum bellowed. "How could you forget something like that?"

"I didn't know it was important! She didn't say what she was letting you down *about*. I just thought you'd invited her for tea." Jess looked cross.

Mum shook her head. She got out her phone. "It doesn't matter," she said. "I'll ring work and ask them to change the date."

"I'm fourteen," Jess said. "I can look after George."

"I'm not leaving you here by yourselves," Mum said. "There'd be a herd of wildebeest in the garden by the time I got back."

I scowled at her. "It's not like we haven't got the room," I said.

"Can't Marta keep an eye on us?" Jess said. "She's only downstairs."

Mum shook her head. "I can't ask someone I've never met to look after my children. It wouldn't be right."

There was a gasp from Mildred. She jumped to her feet. "Tell you what, Fiona. We'll do it. Let *us* look after George and Jess."

My mouth fell open in horror.

Absolutely no *way*.

"I couldn't possibly—" Mum began.

"We'd *love* to help out." Mildred beamed. "I mean, we'd hardly have to do anything. We'd just be here to provide snacks and get them out if there's a fire."

Mum looked worried. "I don't know—"

"Do say yes." Mildred reached over and ruffled my hair. "They'll be no trouble."

I calmed myself down. I had nothing to worry about. Mum would *never* say yes.

"It's ten days," Mum said. "Are you sure?"

"Absolutely, Fiona. We *adore* children." She nudged Muriel, hard. "Don't we, Muriel?"

"Oh yes." Muriel nodded earnestly.

"You won't need to worry about a thing." Mildred gave an excited clap. "This will be a complete treat."

"OK then," Mum said, giving in. "That's wonderful. Thank you *so* much."

I stared at Mum, aghast.

How could she!

83

Mildred and Muriel were *horrible*. They might have told her they liked children, but I knew they didn't!

Why would they even offer?

"George?" Jess sidled over.

"What?" I glared at her. It was her fault we'd ended up with the two worst babysitters in the world.

She checked to make sure Mildred and Muriel weren't listening. "The ruby," she whispered.

"What about it?"

"*They* might think it's on Hornswagg, but if I had a valuable ring, I wouldn't bury it on an island."

"Wouldn't you?"

"No way." Jess shook her head.

I blinked. "You think it's here?"

She nodded. "Yes, I do. *Finders keepers*, they said. If anyone needs something priceless it's *me*. I have a lifetime of race suits to pay for."

I stared at her in excitement. "I'll help look," I said. "We could go fifty-fifty?"

Jess thought about it. "I guess half of priceless is still quite a lot," she said. "It's a deal."

I was woken the next morning by a squeal of brakes. For a moment I didn't know where I was, but then I remembered I'd taken my duvet into the crow's nest and fallen asleep under the stars.

Surely it couldn't be Mildred and Muriel? Not already. The sun was barely up! I grabbed Miss Smallbone's spyglass and peered down.

It *was* them. A battered Rolls-Royce was reversing through the archway at the front of the house with a pile of luggage strapped to the roof. I stared in horror. I thought they were babysitting, not moving in! I could see hatboxes and trunks – and was that a *foot spa*?

The car wouldn't fit through with all the stuff on top and there was a sudden crunch, followed by shouting. Mildred got out the passenger side and bellowed instructions, but it was no good. Muriel had to drive back out and park along the kerb.

She got out looking huffy, and craned her neck towards the house.

I ducked. They weren't going to make me carry all their stuff. No way. I shuffled round to the other side of the crow's nest so they wouldn't be able to see me. I wasn't going down until they'd brought it all in.

Meanwhile, I'd use the spyglass to check out the garden.

It was a good garden. A *really* good one. It had a high

wall all the way round and a lot of trees, so even though we were in the middle of a city, no one could see in from outside. Right at the back, mostly hidden by a bush, was a gate in the wall. I hadn't noticed it before. It led to another bit of garden, with a vegetable patch and a shed. That, I thought, would be *perfect* for my llama. If the bush grew a bit more, Mum wouldn't even notice I had one!

I swept the spyglass around to the fire escape. Dr Gupta was heading up to the attics holding a bucket. Maybe she'd been to collect the eggs? Miserable old bat. She hadn't even come to say hello when we moved in.

I crawled back across to check on Mildred and Muriel. They'd unstrapped most of their cases and were heaving them up the steps. Jess must have come back from early morning training, because she was helping.

She didn't look very pleased about that.

I sat back. Another ten minutes should do it. After that I'd head downstairs and pretend I was surprised to see them.

Then I heard a blood-curdling scream.

FOURTEEN

I always miss the fun stuff.

By the time *I* got there, Jess was pushing a forlorn-looking Boris towards the kitchen. "He only came to say hello," she said. "Muriel went crazy. I'll put him in the garden for now."

I went to help Muriel up off the floor. Her fascinator had slipped behind her ear, and her face was shiny from lick.

"That dreadful animal," she sobbed. "He attacked me. Why on earth would Mary choose such a creature? What's wrong with a poodle?"

Mildred shoved a vanity case into my arms. "Where were you?" she huffed. "We were ringing the doorbell for ages. We had to bring most of this in ourselves."

"I was asleep," I lied. "It is quite early. I think Mum went to the supermarket."

"Well, you're here now." Mildred sniffed. She peered up the staircase. "Where are we?"

"Second floor," I said. Mum had chosen the room as it had two beds and a big wardrobe. It was a painted a horrible green and the best thing was that it was miles away from mine. "I'll show you."

"Wait, George." Muriel trotted over. She draped an armful of ballgowns over the case I was already holding. "These will need to be pressed, dear. Then hung up."

"Once you've done that, you can bring up the rest of our things." Mildred gave me a friendly pat.

I was just about to make an excuse – but annoyingly, I couldn't, as Mum walked in with the shopping. She would have been really surprised to hear I had a violin lesson in twenty minutes, as I don't play the violin.

"Oh, well done, George, for helping," she said when she saw me. "Hello, you two." She waved enthusiastically at Mildred and Muriel. "You're lovely and early. Let me put the groceries away and I'll make you a cup of tea."

"Music to my ears." Muriel clasped her hands. "I'll

need extra sugar, mind. I'm in shock. I was attacked by Mary's dog. *Hideous* creature."

"I'd forgotten you two didn't get along." Mum looked apologetic. "I'll have a word with Jess and make sure she keeps him out of your way."

Where was Jess, anyway? She hadn't come back. She was such a skiver.

"Show them their room, George." Mum stuck her head back into the hall.

"Ooh yes, do, George." Muriel popped a toilet bag on top of her gowns. "I can't wait."

"It's this way." I could hardly see I was carrying so much stuff. I staggered up the stairs. "Here you go." I held open the door.

Muriel gave an excited squeal. "You've put us in Father's room! We were never allowed in as children. He was very strict."

"Where's *your* father, George?" Mildred pushed past me. "I notice you don't have one."

I blinked.

"Is he dead?" Muriel asked.

I thought about telling them he was a spy, working undercover at Buckingham Palace, but I couldn't be bothered.

"He works on a cruise ship," I said.

"Gracious." Mildred tittered. "Does he sing? How glamorous."

"He's an engineer," I said.

"Oh." Mildred lost interest. She seemed pleased by the room, at least. "There's *plenty* of space for our things, Mildred." She turned to me. "George? If you could make sure we have fresh sheets and pillowcases daily – and I do like a little vase of flowers on the dresser."

"I'll make a note." I dumped Muriel's dresses on one of the beds. "Anything else?"

"A plate of biscuits?" Muriel suggested. "Doughnuts if you have any? Or more of those lovely muffins?"

"And we'll take our morning tea at nine thirty, followed by a cocktail at eleven," Mildred instructed.

I stared at them. "This isn't a hotel," I said.

Muriel laughed and gave me a little push. "Silly boy. We're your *guests*," she said. "*Guests*. It would be *rude* for us to make free in your kitchen."

I stared at them and wondered if Marta was back. I could go and hide down there? I didn't care that I hadn't met her. She'd have to be one of Mum's axe murderers to be worse than these two. In fact, I decided, I'd hide down there even if she wasn't. I'd pretend I was going for the rest of the cases, and I wouldn't come back.

"George?"

I checked my watch. "Oh, I'm sorry. Is it time for your cocktail?"

"Silly." Mildred reached into her handbag. "I bought a card for your mother." She pulled it out and held it up. It said CONGRATULATIONS ON YOUR PROMOTION. "Muriel and I have already written in it – we thought you might like to as well?"

She offered me a pen.

It was nice of them to think of Mum, I guess. I signed my name, then handed it back.

Muriel flung open the wardrobe. She let out a cry. "Oh look, Mildred. I remember Father wearing this." She admired a moth-eaten coat. "You can hang my frocks in here, George. We'll go and take tea with your mother."

I stared after them. How could I bear them for ten days?

I picked up Muriel's dresses and bundled them on to the floor of the wardrobe. She could iron them herself.

I went to slam the door – but just as I did, I noticed something odd on the back panel, behind the coat.

Was that *writing*?

FIFTEEN

I climbed in for a better look.

There, behind the old coat, on the back of the wardrobe, someone had scrawled the Smallbone family tree. There were dates of birth and dates of death and gruesome descriptions of how they'd died.

I traced it all the way down to Mildred, Muriel and Mary – and Martin. His name had been scribbled out. His dad must have been so mad to do that. All because he ran away.

I wondered where he was now. I could try and track him down? I bet he'd be pleased to hear from me. I could invite him over to Hogweed Hall and we could talk about Miss Smallbone and he might even know about the terrible thing Sidney Smallbone had done?

I started to back out but my foot got caught in one of Muriel's voluminous skirts. I had to twist round to untangle myself, and as I did there was a crack and something gave way beneath me.

Oops.

I pushed Muriel's dresses aside to view the damage.

Oh.

I hadn't broken anything, like I'd thought.

I'd dislodged a panel in the wardrobe floor.

And there was something underneath.

I pulled the panel out for a better look. Oh. It was just a load of old books. Why would anyone hide books in a wardrob—

Books.

I grabbed one and flipped it open. The pages were yellow and cracked and covered in tiny spidery writing.

I let out a squeak.

I'd found Sidney Smallbone's journals!

I could find out what he did! I flicked through the pages.

"George, dear," Mildred bellowed from downstairs. "What *are* you doing? I almost broke my neck tripping over Muriel's hatbox. Do hurry and get things moved upstairs."

I scowled. I'd have to look properly when I had more time. I put the journal back along with the panel and Muriel's ballgowns, and slid out into the bedroom.

"What are you doing?"

I almost had a heart attack. "Jess!" I glared at her. "Don't sneak up like that. Where have you been?"

"I wondered where *you* were," she said. "And now I'm *here*, I'm wondering what you were doing in the wardrobe."

"I found Sidney's journals," I said.

"That was quick." Jess looked impressed. "Did you find out what he did?"

"I hardly had time to read them, did I?" I huffed. "Mildred and Muriel could come up any minute." I turned to go.

"Wait." Jess picked something up from the floor. "Where did this come from?" She held out a piece of parchment, folded in two. "It looks really old."

I took it. It must have fallen out of the diary. The parchment was old and brittle, and bits flaked from the edges as I smoothed it out.

"Let's see." Jess craned her neck.

"It's a map," I said.

Jess gasped. "It's not just *any* old map, George."

95

"Isn't it?"

"No. Look at it. It's the one Mildred and Muriel were talking about. The one Sidney put in a safe place and lost."

I blinked at her. "The map of the island?"

"Yes." Jess gave a little skip. "I can't believe we've found it. If the ruby isn't in the house – then next stop, Hornswagg."

I stared at her. "And how would *we* get there, exactly?"

Jess shrugged. "There's always a way, George."

"George?" It was Mum's turn to shout. "What *are* you doing?"

I put the map in my pocket and we slunk down to the kitchen. Mum was sitting with Mildred and going through lists, explaining about homework and washing and bedtimes.

"I'll go and check Boris is OK," Jess said. "Poor thing, stuck out in the garden. He must wonder what he's done wrong." She glared at Muriel and let herself out the back.

Muriel was chomping her way through a large piece of Battenberg. "Finished with the luggage?" she said to me brightly.

I sat down next to her. "I'm having a break," I said. "I'll do the rest in a minute."

"What a helpful boy you are." She beamed at me.

I beamed back. I wondered if this was a good time to ask about Martin, their missing brother.

"More cake?" I offered her the plate.

"Don't mind if I do." She fell on it.

"Muriel," I said. "Did you and Mildred have any other siblings, or was it just Mary?"

"Oh no." Muriel shook her head. "Not just Mary. There was Martin. Dim as a burnt-out bulb. He didn't get on with Father."

"Why not?" I asked.

Muriel tittered. "Father had *expectations*," she said. "Martin was ... now how can I put it nicely... There was nothing he was *good* at. Fell off his pony, crashed the dog cart – could barely read, let alone add a simple sum."

He sounded like me. "What happened to him?" I asked.

"He ran away to sea." Mildred joined the conversation. "Your age, he was, George. Father was *furious*. I don't blame him. All that money he'd spent on posh schools. We'd moved on from pirating, you see."

"He signed up as cabin boy on the *Black Sea Dog*." Muriel brushed bits of Battenberg from her blouse. "We weren't allowed to mention his name after that. Father said he was a disgrace."

Mum looked horrified. "Poor Martin," she said. "Are you still in touch?"

Muriel tipped sugar into her tea. "We found out his ship was scuppered not long after. The whole crew walked the plank. They were miles from shore. There's no way he'd have made it."

"But they never found his body," I said.

Mildred's head snapped round. She gave me a gimlet stare. "And how do you know that?" she said, coldly.

"I overheard you," I explained. "At the funeral."

"Did you now?" Mildred's eyes narrowed.

"We all wanted a happy ending, George dear." Muriel patted my shoulder. "But the sad fact is, Martin drowned."

The back door slammed and Jess came in. Muriel gave a mew of fear. "Where's that awful dog?"

"Still outside," Jess said. "He can't stay there for ever, though. You'll have to get used to him."

"Shall I take him for a walk?" I asked. "I could have a go at teaching him tricks."

Jess looked doubtful. "I don't think he's particularly bright," she said. "If you're going to train him, I'd start with the basics. You know, like walking to heel and not jumping up."

Muriel looked approving. "What a good idea," she said. "Nasty slobbery creature."

Jess scowled at her. "He's only being *friendly* when he does that, actually," she said. "He doesn't realize it upsets people. He's a *dog*."

"More tea?" Mum offered round the pot.

Jess gave Muriel a glare and passed me Boris's lead.

"Take some treats," she said. "You won't get far without those. They're on the side."

"OK," I said. "Thanks."

The treats were small and brown and bone shaped. They didn't smell very good, but Boris liked them. I stuck a handful in my pocket and headed out.

SIXTEEN

If I'm being honest, Boris wasn't the greatest dog to walk.
It felt like *he* was in charge, not me. He almost pulled me
off my feet every time he saw a cat, or a squirrel – then
stopped for a sit-down any time he felt like one.

The sooner I started his training, the better.

We were on the common now, away from traffic. I
unclipped his lead and set
off along the path. "Heel,
Boris," I said. *"Heel."*

Boris looked up from
under his shaggy
eyebrows and
wagged his tail.
He seemed

perfectly happy to trot along beside me. I gave him one of the bone-shaped treats and a pat. This wasn't as hard as I thought. "Good boy, Boris," I said. "*Good* boy."

I carried on walking. "Morning," I said to a woman coming towards me, nodding at her, like a proper dog walker.

She looked at the lead in my hand, then pointed back the way I'd come. "Is that your dog?" she said.

I was about to say, *No, my dog is here, with his obedient nose to my heel* – but I thought it best to look, just in case.

"Is it?" she asked.

"Yes." I watched as Boris disappeared into the distance. "Yes. I think it might be."

I spent a long time looking for Boris but I couldn't find him, so I went home. Jess went nuts when I told her. "He slipped his collar," I lied. "Sorry."

"I can't believe you lost him," she said. "Suppose he runs in front of a car or eats a child?" She snatched the lead from me and stomped off down the hall. "I'll go and look. You stay here in case he gets back. Text me if he does."

I slunk out into the garden. I couldn't believe Jess had been so cross with me. It wasn't *my* fault Boris wasn't trained. He was *her* dog. I'd done my best.

"Hi, George." Mum waved at me from the henhouse.

I went over.

"Any eggs?" I said.

She shook her head. "No. Not one. I don't understand it. With this many chickens, you'd think there'd be loads."

"Dr Gupta was down here this morning," I said. "I expect she's collected them."

"I'll have to get up earlier," Mum huffed. "Beat her to it." She started walking back towards the house. "What do you think digs all these holes in the lawn? A rabbit?"

"Jess and I think someone's looking for treasure," I said.

Mum laughed. "You two are funny."

She'd see when we dug up that ruby. "What time are you leaving?" I asked.

Mum checked her watch. "My taxi will be here in an hour," she said. "I better bring my bags down."

"Where are Mildred and Muriel?" I asked.

"They've gone for a nap," Mum said. "They were tired after moving the rest of the stuff up to their room." She looked at me. "I thought you were supposed to do that."

I scowled. "Don't blame me. Jess said she'd take it up if I took Boris for a walk."

"Well, she must have forgotten."

Honestly. Jess was *so* annoying. I'd planned to get Sidney's journals from the wardrobe this afternoon. If Mildred and Muriel were snoring away in their room, I wouldn't be able to.

"Have you seen her?" Mum asked. "I must wish her luck for the championship before I go."

"Maybe she went out with Boris?" I said. I didn't mention I'd lost him.

Mum shook her head. "Boris is over there."

I looked where she was pointing. Oh yes. *There* he was. Lolling on the patio, tongue out, looking like he hadn't a care in the world.

Mum headed for the house. "I'll go and find her."

I waited for the back door to shut before giving Boris a piece of my mind. "No more treats for you," I said. "You're a disgrace."

Boris didn't care what I thought. He gave me a disparaging look, and yawned. It was then I noticed an envelope tucked into his collar. I peered closer.

It had my name on it.

I tried to grab it, but Boris thought I was playing, and kept biting my arm with his shaggy jaws. I told him to stop several times, but he took no notice of anything I said *at all*. In the end I had to get the bone treats out.

While he was distracted, I snatched the envelope and stared at it.

Was that Marta's writing?

"Hey."

Jess was back. She stomped over, scowling. "You were supposed to text me if he turned up," she said.

I scowled back. "And *you* were supposed to take up the rest of Mildred and Muriel's bags," I said.

"I was *going* to but I'm glad I didn't," Jess said. "The deal was you'd take him for a walk, not lose him."

"It's not my fault your dog is completely untrainable," I huffed. I turned my back on her.

"What's that?" Jess had seen the envelope in my hand.

"Nothing to do with *you*," I said. Jess tried to look, but I moved so she couldn't.

I opened the flap and pulled out a scrap of paper.

George

I need to tell you something. A secret. Meet me by the shed at midnight.

Come on your own.

Marta

PS Destroy this.

"Who's it from?" Jess asked.

"Marta," I said. "She heard I really liked her biscuits. It's the recipe."

"I don't believe you," Jess said. "Let me see." She held out her hand.

"Nope." I scrunched up the note and popped it in my mouth. I was fed up with her bossing me about and thinking she was in charge. I chewed loudly.

"You're such a baby." Jess shook her head.

"Whatever," I said. Then I stomped off. The note had been harder to swallow than I thought, so I spat it out round the corner, where Jess couldn't see me. It wasn't *completely* destroyed like Marta had asked, but it was unlikely anyone would want to uncrumple it.

I wondered what she wanted to tell me. It must be important. Maybe she knew where that ruby was? I hoped so, because if I found it first it'd really annoy Jess.

I stayed away from Jess all afternoon. I said goodbye to Mum and I went up to the crow's nest and spent ages looking at things through the spyglass. It was fun until I got hungry. I checked my jacket for snacks, but I only found the map to Hornswagg, Boris's bone-shaped treats – and the flyer for the musical the man in the shop had given me. I was just about to make it into a paper aeroplane when I recognized someone in one of the photographs.

Mr Wickom.

Ahaha. He looked ever so funny in costume.

It suited him.

SEVENTEEN

At eleven forty-five that night, Hogweed Hall was dark.
It wasn't *just* dark. It was pitch black. There wasn't any
moonlight and I didn't dare put a torch on, in case
someone saw.

I crept down the corridor. Every time a floorboard
creaked, I jumped out of my skin.

I almost wished I'd invited Jess.

I tiptoed down the stairs and through to the kitchen.
I'd been planning to take Boris with me, for moral
support, but he wasn't there.

Just me, then.

I let myself out the back door.

The garden wasn't inviting at this time of night.
There were weird shapes everywhere, and an owl kept

hooting. My eyes had got used to the dark, but even so, it was hard to see where the holes in the lawn were. I'd have to be careful not to trip.

I crept toward the gate in the back wall.

I'd barely made it across the patio when I heard a noise. I turned, but there was no one there.

I told myself off for being silly. What was I scared of? The house looked friendly enough behind me. There was a dim glow in the attic. Dr Gupta must be working late.

Eh? A movement caught my eye.

I froze.

Was that someone on the fire escape?

Someone in a long dark coat?

No. It couldn't be. It was just a shadow.

Get a grip, George.

I carried on across the garden.

The latch on the gate made a tiny clink as I slipped through it.

The shed loomed ahead of me.

And there was a crack of a twig behind me.

"Boo," said a voice.

I thought I was going to die of fright, but I didn't, I just made a little choking noise.

"Don't panic." Jess stepped out from behind a large shrub. "It's only me."

"You almost gave me a heart attack," I hissed.

"Sorry," Jess said.

I bet she *wasn't*. "You picked up Marta's note, didn't you?" I glared at her, but being dark, I don't know if she got the benefit.

"Ew, no. Not after you'd chewed it. I read it over your shoulder."

"Oh." I couldn't see her but I *bet* she was smirking. "Marta didn't invite *you*," I said. "She invited *me*."

"So why did she want to meet you here?" Jess asked. "And not her flat? Suppose it wasn't from her? Suppose it was from someone else?"

"Who, exactly?"

"An axe murderer who's annoyed that you inherited Hogweed?" Jess suggested.

Oh. I hadn't thought of that.

"Someone's coming," Jess whispered.

The gate chinked, and footsteps rustled through the grass towards us.

I squeaked in terror.

Luckily, the moon came out before I fainted from fear. It *was* Marta. I recognized her shawl from the flat.

She had Boris with her.

He sniffed us out immediately. He was as pleased to see us as he always was. We both went flying.

"I thought I told you to come on your own, George?" Marta sounded annoyed as she loomed above me.

I let out a strangled squawk

It wasn't Marta.

It was the ghost of Miss Smallbone.

EIGHTEEN

Jess was braver than me.

She scrambled to her feet. "Hello," she said. "What a surprise."

"*You* weren't supposed to be here." Miss Smallbone's ghost sounded annoyed.

"It's a good thing I am." Jess sounded annoyed too. "Look how scared he is." She pointed at me. "He's only eleven."

Miss Smallbone's ghost looked abashed. "Sorry, George."

I tried to say "That's OK" but it came out as a bleat.

"I think you need to explain yourself," Jess said.

The ghost scowled. "This is all your mother's fault," she said. "If it wasn't for her, I wouldn't be here."

"Mum's fault?" I got up. "How is it Mum's fault you're dead?"

Jess looked at me. "Miss Smallbone's not dead, George."

I blinked at her, then at Miss Smallbone.

Not dead?

"You didn't think I was a ghost, did you?" Miss Smallbone snorted.

I stared at her some more. "Having been to your *memorial* service, then *yes*, I did."

Miss Smallbone cackled. "Well, I'm not."

I gave her a cold look. "What a mean trick."

"It wasn't a *trick*," Miss Smallbone huffed. "My plan was brilliant. It didn't start to go wrong until this morning, when I saw my worm-witted sisters trotting up the drive. What on earth was your mother thinking, inviting murderers to stay?"

"Murderers?" Jess took a step back.

"That's why I'm dead." Miss Smallbone nodded.

"You just said you weren't," I said.

"I *would* be if their plan had worked," Miss Smallbone said. "They tried hard enough."

"They tried to *murder* you?" I blinked.

"They certainly did." Miss Smallbone scowled. "I

decided to fake my own death. Let them think they'd succeeded. Mildred and Millicent might *seem* like fawning old ladies, but underneath, they're murderous, backstabbing cockroaches."

"Are they?" I glanced at the house in horror.

"I think we're safe enough out here." Miss Smallbone patted my arm. "Now, George, do you want to hear this? It's not pleasant."

"I'm not a baby," I said.

"OK, if you're sure," Miss Smallbone said. "Now where shall I start?"

"The beginning, perhaps?" Jess suggested.

Miss Smallbone frowned. "I'm just not sure where the beginning *is*." She thought for a moment. "It was after I invited Dr Gupta to set up her lab in my attic. Everything was going swimmingly – then an attempt was made on my life. A rock tumbled off a wall, just missing my head. It made the *Hamfield Gazette*."

"Are you sure it wasn't an accident?" I said.

"The *Gazette* implied that, but it was *not*." Miss Smallbone huffed. "A month or two later, a *second* attempt was made. I'd cooked a delicious gooseberry crumble and left it in the pantry. The next day, I noticed something."

"What?" I asked.

"A mouse. Dead. Lying next to the dish. *Now*, I thought to myself, *my cooking isn't that bad!*"

I thought back to the curry biscuits and gravy buns. *That* was a matter of opinion, I felt.

"I bagged up some of the crumble and took it to Dr Gupta to analyse." Miss Smallbone scowled. "What do you think she found?"

We stared at her. "What?" I said.

"RAT POISON!"

"Rat poison?" I blinked at her.

"Yes." Her eyes flashed. "*Rat poison.*"

"And you think it was Mildred and Muriel?"

"I *know* it was them," Miss Smallbone snapped. "Do you want to know HOW I knew it was them?"

"Please," Jess said, politely.

Miss Smallbone reached inside her shawl. She pulled out a sheet of paper. "The day after, I found this in my desk. I suspect it'd been there a while."

"What is it?" I asked.

"It's a will." Miss Smallbone was calmer now. "*My* will. Would you like to look at it?"

"OK." Jess took it. She flicked on her torch and ran her eyes down the page. "Oh." She looked up. "It leaves

Hogweed Hall to Mildred and Muriel."

"What?" I snatched it and stared at it. "How?"

"It's a forgery, of course." Miss Smallbone sounded triumphant. "They planted it, then tried to kill me."

"That's terrible," Jess said.

I was finding it hard to take in.

Murder.

Mum had asked murderers to babysit us.

Miss Smallbone went on. "Mildred *always* wanted Hogweed Hall. After Martin ran away, she thought she would inherit, being the eldest. The night she discovered Hogweed had been left to me, she took Muriel and stormed into the night. When I went out the next morning, there was only one M above the door. They'd chiselled the other two off."

"Why murder you *now*, though?" Jess asked. "And not back then?"

"No idea." Miss Smallbone sniffed. "Mildred always did hold a grudge. I expect the injustice festered and got too much."

"Maybe they've run out of money?" I suggested.

"Father left them loads," Miss Smallbone said. "They can't have spent it *all*."

"Did you report them?" Jess asked.

Miss Smallbone shook her head. "I came up with a *far* better plan." She paused. "Which it *was*, until your mum messed it up."

"You pretended to be dead," I said. "How is that a good plan?"

"You don't understand, George," Miss Smallbone scowled at me. "I'm working on something. Something important. I can't die until it's complete. Don't you see? If Mildred and Muriel think I'm out the picture, I'm safe."

Oh. That made sense.

"I had to make it convincing, of course. I hired Mr Wickom from the local dramatic society. He's not really a solicitor." She looked at me. "Were they cross I left everything to you?"

"Very," I said.

"Oh *good*." Miss Smallbone clapped her hands.

"Is Hogweed Hall still mine?" I asked.

"Yes." Miss Smallbone nodded. "I wanted you to have it. The deeds are in your name."

Jess went pale. "So," she said, slowly. "George now owns a house that Mildred was prepared to kill for?" She stared at Miss Smallbone. "Is he in danger?"

"Gracious." Miss Smallbone blinked. "I hadn't thought about that."

My insides went cold. "Am I next on their list?"

"I wouldn't worry," Miss Smallbone said, chirpily. "They'd need your signature to forge another will. Just don't sign anything."

Jess said she had to get up early and we should go back to the house.

"What happens when Mum comes home?" I asked Miss Smallbone. "If she sees you, she'll recognize you."

"No need to panic, George. My work with Dr Gupta is almost complete." Miss Smallbone pushed open the cellar door. "As soon as it is, I'll be off. I have a trip planned."

"Dr Gupta knows you're alive?" I stared at her.

"Oh yes," Miss Smallbone said. "*She* didn't think much of my plan – but *she* wasn't the one being murdered, was she?"

"What *are* you working on?" Jess asked.

"It's a secret," Miss Smallbone said. "I'll tell you when we've finished."

I was going to ask for a hint, but she looked at her watch and said she was exhausted from all the explaining

118

and was going to bed.

"And I've got early morning training," Jess said. "Come on, George."

On the way to my room, I looked out the window.

Dr Gupta was in the garden.

Digging.

NINETEEN

I went and sat on my bed.

I was pleased Miss Smallbone was alive, but I was also annoyed with her. It's not very nice to pretend you're dead, even if you give someone your house. I was also cross she wouldn't tell me what she was working on with Dr Gupta.

They might be friends, but Dr Gupta was *definitely* up to something she shouldn't be. What was she digging for? The ruby? Was *everyone* looking for the ruby? And Mildred and Muriel ... *murderers*? At least I'd been warned to be on my guard, and not to sign anything.

Oh.

I had a sudden vision of Mildred passing me a pen.

A chill ran down my spine.

Mum's card.

I'd signed it.

Mildred and Muriel had my signature.

My door didn't lock, so I dragged a chair over and balanced a whole load of stuff on it. If anyone came in it would fall with a crash and give me time to grab the lamp and hit them with it. Then I got back into bed and lay there, staring at the ceiling.

I didn't like being scared. Tomorrow, I might tell Mildred and Muriel they could keep the house. Then they wouldn't need to murder me.

I *was* woken by a crash, but when I shot out of bed, the chair and everything on it was still there. I pulled on my dressing gown and followed the bangs and thuds to the kitchen.

Mildred and Muriel had decided to spring-clean. "It'll be a wonderful surprise for your mother," Muriel trilled from inside a cupboard. "We're going to have a really good sort-out for her."

"That's very kind of you," I said. "I'm sure she'll be pleased." I was feeling braver this morning. Mildred didn't look particularly murderous in her apron – though after the things I'd heard last night, I was going to keep a very close eye on her.

"I made some porridge," Muriel called from the pantry. "It's on the stove."

I let out a squeak of terror. I bet they'd put poison in it.

Mildred bustled over. "We promised your mother you'd eat properly." She slopped some porridge into a bowl. "Here you go." She popped it on the table.

I pulled myself together. "Why, thank you," I said. "How *kind*. Could I trouble you for a glass of juice?"

"Of course."

The minute her back was turned I whipped Mum's flowers out of the vase in front of me and tipped the porridge in. Mildred seemed surprised when she saw my empty bowl. "More?" she asked. I held up my hand. "That was delicious, but no thanks."

I went to find Jess.

"There was poison in the porridge," I said. "I mean, I don't know for sure, as I didn't eat it, but I bet there was."

"It tasted all right to me," Jess said. "I had loads."

I stared at her. "Are you feeling OK?"

"Perfectly well," Jess said. "Is there something you wanted? I've got to go swimming."

"I accidentally gave them my signature," I said.

"Suppose they've forged a will and kill me while you're out?"

"I'm sure they won't," Jess said.

"How do you know?" I sat on the bed.

"I was thinking last night," Jess said. "Mildred and Muriel don't want the house."

"Don't they?" I looked at her in surprise.

Jess shook her head. "It's the ruby they're after. You heard them. If they found it, they'd be the richest women in Europe. They couldn't turn the house upside down while Miss Smallbone was here." She smirked. "They don't want Hogweed Hall. They want the map to Hornswagg."

"That's why they offered to babysit?"

"Yep." Jess picked up her swim stuff. "And that's why they're downstairs going through the cupboards."

"I've got nothing to worry about?"

"Not a thing." She headed for the door.

I stared after her.

I hoped she was right.

Suppose she wasn't?

TWENTY

I wasn't convinced that Jess was taking the threat to my life seriously enough. There'd have been a huge fuss if *she* was the one about to be murdered. I decided to find Miss Smallbone and let *her* know I'd accidentally given Mildred and Muriel my signature. She'd know what to do. Maybe we could come up with a plan to get rid of them?

I snuck down to the flat in the cellar. Boris was there, snoring in front of the fireplace. He heard me and opened an eye, then shut it again. There was no sign of Miss Smallbone. Maybe she'd gone to see Dr Gupta?

There was a crash from overhead. It sounded like Mildred and Millicent had moved their search to the parlour. This could be a good time to get Sidney's diaries? I crept back up to the kitchen and across the hall.

I wasn't quiet enough. Muriel stuck her head out. She had a scarf tied around her curls. "George?" she trilled. "A cup of tea would be nice. Tidying is thirsty work."

"Of course, Muriel," I said. "I'll put the kettle on."

"Maybe a small snack as well?"

"Of course." I pretended to head for the kitchen, then swerved up the stairs to their bedroom.

The door was locked.

I gave it a kick. This was *so* annoying. At this rate I'd *never* find out what Sidney had done. There were too many secrets in this house. I scowled. I'd go up to the lab. I'd *make* them tell me what they were doing up there.

I crept up the rest of the stairs and into the attic corridor. There was no one about – but a breeze ruffled my hair. The fire escape must be open. Maybe Dr Gupta had gone to collect the eggs? I tiptoed along the passage, then stopped. Oh my. The lab door was ajar! I peered carefully round it.

Empty.

I slipped inside.

Wow. I blinked in the bright lights. It really *was* a proper lab. There was no sign of the old trunks and stuffed parrots that'd been here when I came to tea. The walls were gleaming white, and two steel tables ran the length of the room. The only thing that looked out of place were some old-looking books on the table.

I flipped one open. Birds. That wasn't very exciting. I shut it again and moved further down the room.

At the end were two enormous tanks.

Now *they* looked interesting. I crept over and peered in.

Eh?

Eggs?

Loads of them. On a series of trays, which rotated under a lamp.

Incubators?

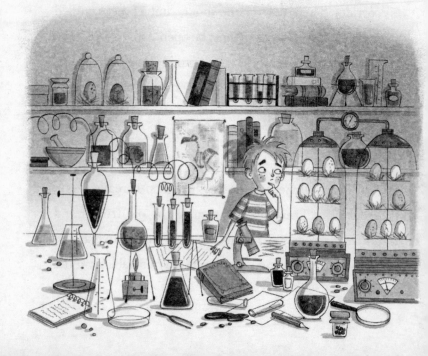

Was this Miss Smallbone's project? Hatching out hens?

Why was it such a secret? I didn't understand. Where *was* Miss Smallbon— Oh.

Footsteps. Behind me.

I turned around.

Dr Gupta stood in front of me holding a bucket. "What do you think you're doing?" she raged. "No one's allowed in here."

"George?" A panel in the wall slid back and Miss Smallbone popped out from the secret staircase. "I'm sure I told you to stay out of the attics."

"No," I said. "You definitely didn't. What are you doing with all those eggs?

Dr Gupta looked furious. "We're working on something incredibly important – and you shouldn't be here."

"You're breeding chickens," I said. "How is that important?"

Miss Smallbone shook her head. "It's not as simple as that. The eggs—"

"Miss *Smallbone*," Dr Gupta interrupted. "We agreed *no one* must know."

"I wasn't going to say anything." Miss Smallbone sniffed.

"Can't I help?" I said. "I like science. You don't have to tell me what you're doing."

"No." Dr Gupta stood firm.

"Please?"

"Oh, let him feed the chicks." Miss Smallbone said.

"Yay!" I gave a hop.

Dr Gupta scowled, but she held out the bucket. "Take these. They're freshly dug."

I took it and peered inside.

Oh.

Worms.

That explained the holes in the lawn. How disappointing. I'd been *positive* Dr Gupta was up to no good.

"This way." Miss Smallbone headed for a door that led to another part of the attic. I followed with the bucket.

"Don't tell him a *thing*." Dr Gupta glared after us.

"I won't." Miss Smallbone closed the door behind us. "Must keep the heat in," she said. She pointed to a pen under the eaves. "Look how cute they are."

The chicks *were* cute, cheeping away. *Really* cute. I threw in a handful of worms. "Dr Gupta's very bossy," I said.

"She's good at her job," Miss Smallbone said. "A

genius, in fact." She lowered her voice. "But you're right. She *is* bossy."

I stroked one of the chicks. "Please tell me what you're doing."

"If I do," Miss Smallbone said. "You mustn't breathe a word to a living soul."

I almost dropped the bucket. "I won't. I promise."

"And don't tell Dr Gupta I told you. She'd be furious."

I tipped the rest of the worms into the pen. "You can trust me," I said. "I won't say a thing."

Miss Smallbone waved towards the chicks. "All this is down to Sidney Smallbone."

I might have known.

"Back in 1678," Miss Smallbone said, "Sidney readied his ship, *The Windy Pig*, and set off for the West Indies with his bride, Twelve-Toe Tina. They were heading for the Isle of Hornswagg, which Sidney had won in an arm wrestle."

"From John the Pox?" I said.

Miss Smallbone glared at me. "Would you like to tell the story?"

"No," I said. "Sorry."

"Hornswagg was surrounded by rocks. There was only one way through. They managed it, but in doing

129

so, ripped a hole in *The Windy Pig's* hull. They had no choice but to stay on the island until the crew repaired her."

"How long were they stranded for?" I asked.

"Six months. They soon ran out of supplies. They had to live off the land. Coconuts. Mangos. Wild boar." Miss Smallbone shook her head. "Tina turned out to be a wonderful cook. She was very creative. While she was there, she jotted down her recipes in a notebook."

"How nice," I said, politely. I wished she'd hurry up. Dr Gupta might come in and interrupt.

"Unfortunately –" Miss Smallbone's face went dark "– wild boar was not the only thing Sidney and Tina Smallbone developed a taste for."

"No?"

"They started to snare large land birds. Dodos."

"Dodos?" I stared at her. "There were *dodos* on Hornswagg?"

"Yes," Miss Smallbone said. "There *were*. By all accounts they were *delicious*. Sidney and Tina liked their food. It wasn't long before ... before ..."

"Before what?"

"BEFORE THEY'D EATEN EVERY SINGLE ONE," Miss Smallbone bellowed.

I stared at her. "All of them?"

"Yes, George." Miss Smallbone drew a shuddering breath. "My great-great-grandfather, Sidney Smallbone, *ate the very last dodo.*"

I blinked. "Oh."

Miss Smallbone let out a wail. "He stuffed it with kumquats and said it was tasty."

"Blimey," I said.

"I *told* you it was awful." Miss Smallbone pulled out a large hanky and blew her nose. "When I closed that journal, I vowed I wouldn't rest until I'd made amends for his crime."

I looked around. "And you're doing that by breeding chickens?" I asked.

Miss Smallbone snorted. "We're not breeding *chickens.*"

"What *are* you doing, then?" I asked.

Miss Smallbone puffed herself up. "Dr Gupta and I," she said, "are resurrecting the dodo."

TWENTY-ONE

"You're resurrecting the *dodo*?" My eyes almost popped out of my head.

"We certainly are." Miss Smallbone clapped her hands. "Isn't it exciting?"

I blinked at her. "How?"

"You extract DNA from a feather and pop it into an egg. Dr Gupta's an expert." Miss Smallbone glanced towards the door, then lowered her voice. "She's been working towards this her whole life. She was based at the Natural History Museum, but fell out with the curator. That's why I asked her to help. We've been practising with chickens."

I could barely speak. "Wow," I managed.

"It's been tried before," Miss Smallbone said. "But

132

no one had Dr Gupta's experience or ..." She paused. "... dodo DNA."

"You have dodo DNA?" I gawped at her.

"I certainly do," Miss Smallbone trilled. "Remember my hat?"

"The feathery one?"

"Yes."

"Twelve-Toe Tina made that hat when she was stranded on Hornswagg. With *dodo* feathers."

My mouth fell open.

"We'll be using the DNA from those."

I could hardly believe what I was hearing. "That's *amazing*," I said. "Do you think I could film? For my YouTube channel? Because—"

"No!" Miss Smallbone jumped up. "Can you *imagine* what would happen if this got out? We'd be overrun with press."

I blinked. What was wrong with that? Maybe she didn't understand about YouTube? If you got enough views, people sent you free stuff!

I was about to explain, but Miss Smallbone was looking really cross, so I changed the subject. "Have you got any dodo eggs yet?

Miss Smallbone looked shifty. "No."

I gave her a hard stare.

"Oh, all right then." She gave in. "We've done a trial run. There's twelve in the incubator. We used the feathers from Tina's fan." She paused. "Though Dr Gupta was not convinced of their *authenticity*," she said. "She thought they were more likely to have come from a parrot."

"Oh," I said.

"No matter," Miss Smallbone said. "We're preparing another batch tonight – with feathers from the hat this time. They're one hundred percent dodo."

"Can I help?" I begged. "Please?"

"You can fetch the hat." Miss Smallbone said. "Bring it up after tea? Dr Gupta might let you stay."

"Where is it?" I asked.

"In a hatbox," Miss Smallbone said. "Top shelf of the wardrobe in the blue room."

Oh. I blinked. Jess was in the blue room. She'd said she was going to have a clear-out. I hoped she hadn't. Not yet, anyway.

Miss Smallbone looked at me. "Something wrong?" she asked.

"Not a thing," I lied. I followed her back into the lab. "I just remembered I have a violin lesson in twenty minutes. I better go."

"Is he off?" Dr Gupta was flipping through *Everything You Need to Know About Dodos*. "Jolly good. I hope you didn't tell him anything."

"Not a word. Use the secret stairs, George." Miss Smallbone waved towards the fireplace. "Take a left at the first fork you come to. It leads to your bedroom. Don't go right, you'll end up in Mildred and Muriel's. The panels slide. It's all quite easy."

"OK." I climbed through the opening.

The stairs were narrow and dark, but I felt my way down as fast as I could and slid open the panel and scrambled through it into my room. Then I ran across the landing to Jess's and flung open her wardrobe.

I was too late.

The wardrobe was no longer packed with dusty old boxes and moth-eaten coats. It was clean and tidy and Jess's clothes hung in neat rows. There was no sign of the hatbox. I checked all the drawers and under the bed just in case.

I sat down in despair.

What was I going to tell Miss Smallbone?

I jumped as the door flew open. "Why are you here?" Jess slung her swim kit on the floor. "Tummy ache from the poison porridge?"

"Miss Smallbone's hat." I stood up. "It was in the wardrobe. What did you do with it?"

"I took it to the charity shop," Jess said. "Along with six moth-eaten fur coats and a seventeenth-century raccoon-tail undergarment."

"Miss Smallbone wants it back," I said.

"Really?" Jess looked surprised. "I doubt anyone bought it. It's the shop near the church. Ring them and see." She threw me her phone.

I dialled the number. If they still had it, I could run and get it and Miss Smallbone would never kno— Oh. The charity shop man said it had gone already. Sold first thing. A lady. She was going to a wedding and she'd sat on her own hat in the car ... no, he didn't know who she was. He didn't ask customers for their names and addresses. No, *never*.

"What's the big deal?" Jess asked. "It was ever so old."

"Three hundred and thirty years old, *actually*." I forgot I was sworn to secrecy and told Jess everything.

She didn't even believe me! She laughed! "They can't bring back the dodo," she said. "It's impossible."

"They did it with dinosaurs."

"George, that was a *film*."

"It'll work. They've been practising on chickens. That's why there's so many in the garden."

Jess still looked dubious. I didn't care if she believed me or not. "I need to get that hat back," I said.

"What are you going to do?" Jess asked. "Walk about and see if you can spot it?"

"No. The person bought it for a wedding. I'm going to the church."

"That's quite clever for you," Jess said. "I'll go and get Boris. He could do with a walk."

"Can you hurry?" I said. "I'll wait downstairs."

Mildred and Muriel were crashing about in the parlour. I patted my pocket to check I still had the map. I should probably hide it. I stuck my head round the door. "I'm just popping out," I said.

Mildred gave me a cheery wave "Take care on those busy roads. I wouldn't want to tell your mum you'd had a terrible accident."

Muriel giggled. "See you later, George dear."

They made me uneasy. I wished they'd just leave. Jess *said* I was safe, but she wasn't the one who might be murdered, was she?

A thought crept into my mind.

An *excellent* thought.

Why didn't I let them have the map?

Jess was convinced the ruby was here – but even if it wasn't, we'd never go to Hornswagg to look for it, would we? It was too far away.

Far away would be a good place for Mildred and Muriel to be.

I could put the map somewhere they'd find it. Then they'd pack their stuff and go.

I'd do it now. Their bedroom would be a good place.

I used the secret stairs. I ran up them as fast as I could and scrambled through the panel and looked around. Where should I put it? Back where it was? I opened the wardrobe. Muriel's dresses were still in a heap so I tucked it under those, but left a corner sticking out so it was hard to miss.

Perfect. They'd be gone in no time.

I went down to join Jess.

TWENTY-TWO

It was a big wedding and there were a lot of hats. In the middle of them all was Miss Smallbone's. It was perched on the head of a woman who was bossing everyone about. "Hurry," she bellowed. "Get inside. The car will arrive any minute."

She caught sight of me and Jess, and then she saw Boris. She raced over. "You can't take a dog in," she snapped.

"Don't worry," I said. "We're not guests."

"I love your hat." Jess admired it.

"Thank you." The woman patted it, then lowered her voice. "Don't tell anyone. It was second-hand. It only cost a pound."

"Oh." Jess stepped backwards.

The woman looked startled. "What?"

"Something jumped out of it," Jess said. "A flea, I think."

"A *flea?*" The woman snatched the hat from her head and stared at it in horror.

"I'll give it a brush for you." Jess whipped it from her hand.

"The bride's here." I pointed towards the gate.

"Bum." The woman dashed towards the car that had just pulled up.

"What about your hat?" Jess called.

"Burn it!" the woman called back.

That was clever. I'd *never* have thought of a flea.

We set off for home. Thank goodness I wasn't going to have to face Miss Smallbone without her hat. I held it up. Incredible. I was looking at the feathers of the very last dodo.

Then something hopped out of them.

I normally like insects, but this one came right at me. I didn't even think. I hurled the hat away.

It wouldn't have mattered if we hadn't been walking across a bridge at the time.

We watched the hat sail down the river.

"I didn't realize you'd *actually* seen a flea," I said crossly.

"Didn't you?" Jess said.

"Do you think," I said, "if you swam after it, you could catch it?"

"No," said Jess. "I don't."

We went and sat at a table outside the community centre. Neither of us said anything for a while. The only person who wasn't upset was Boris. He was busy barking at a squirrel.

"You *could* have gone after it," I said.

"I wasn't going to risk my life for a *hat*." Jess sounded cross.

"It wasn't *just* a hat," I said. "It was a dodo." My eyes felt scratchy. "A whole *load* of dodos. Miss Smallbone only left me her house so she could finish her project."

"I know," Jess said. "Do you want an ice cream?"

"No."

We sat in silence for a bit longer. Maybe the hat wasn't so important? After all, Miss Smallbone and Dr Gupta had done a trial run, and there were already twelve eggs in the tank in the attic. Though, according to Miss Smallbone, Dr Gupta had thought the feathers they'd used were from parrots.

"I guess we better go home," Jess said.

I shook my head. "I'm not going back without dodo DNA," I said. I stood up. "Come on."

"Come on where?" Jess followed me, dragging Boris.

"The Natural History Museum."

TWENTY-THREE

The bus driver didn't want to let Boris on. He said he'd take up too many seats and scare the old people. In the end, Jess had to hand over ten pounds. "You can pay me back," she said.

"He's your dog," I said.

"Your idea." She looked out the window. "Why are we going to the Natural History Museum, anyway?"

"There's a dodo exhibition. We'll just take a *tiny* bone, no one will miss it."

"What a *wonderful* plan." Jess clearly didn't think so. "Have you thought about *how* you will take the tiny bone?"

I had to admit I hadn't. "You could create a diversion?" I suggested.

Jess said she wasn't going to get into trouble for a mad old lady's project.

"Please, Jess," I begged her. "We'll be in and out like lightning. I have to do this. I want to bring back the dodo more than *anything*."

She shook her head.

"I'll buy Boris off you. You can get your race suit?"

She scowled. "We'll go in and look," she said. "I'm not promising anything."

The museum was busy and the lady on the desk said there was no way Boris was coming in, even if I *did* know Mr Mason.

In the end we tied his lead to a railing by the souvenir stand. "We won't be long," Jess told him. "Ten minutes at the most. Be good."

Boris wasn't listening. He tried to follow us, then barked loudly when he discovered he couldn't.

I pointed at him sternly. "Stay," I said. "*Stay*."

Boris flumped himself down, then rested his head on his paws. "*See*," I said to Jess. "You have to be firm."

I left him some of the bone treats. He stared after us, but stayed put.

*

I hadn't been to the Natural History Museum in *ages*. The massive Tyrannosaurus rex fossil in the entrance hall was still there. It would have been good to get some DNA from that as well, but when I asked the attendant, he said it was a replica. "Wire and plaster," he said. "There's three more out the back."

"The dodo bones aren't plaster, are they?" I started to worry.

The attendant shook his head. "You can tell the real stuff. It's locked behind glass."

Locked? That was annoying. "Padlock or combination?" I asked, casually.

"Combination." The attendant lowered his voice. "The code is the curator's birthday. It's so we don't forget to buy him a cake." He scowled. "Not that we ever get any."

I pulled a sympathetic face. "Mean," I said.

"Telling me." The attendant walked off with a sniff.

I ran after him. "What was Mr Mason's birthday again?" I asked. "He's a friend of my dad's. I was going to get him a card."

"Didn't know he had any friends." The attendant pulled a face. "Nineteenth December."

"Thanks," I said.

"The dodos are this way." Jess came over with a map. "It was an extra ten pounds to see them. You'll have to pay me back."

"Of course," I lied.

She looked at me. "What's the plan?" she asked.

"The cabinets are locked," I said. "Luckily, I know the combination."

Jess blinked. "Do you? How?"

I tapped my head, as if to indicate genius. "The first four numbers are one nine one two – and the last bit is the year Mr Mason was born."

"Which is?" Jess raised her eyebrows.

Annoyingly, I had to admit I didn't know. Jess didn't think much of that. "Well, you're the one that met him," she said. "How old do you *think* he looked?"

I thought back to his bald head and shiny beige suit. "Sixty?" I guessed. "I'll try that, then the years either side."

"So much for in and out like lightning," Jess huffed. "If you're going to spend hours typing in different codes, we better get a move on." She marched ahead.

I followed her through the crowds. It was ever so busy. Jess was going to have to distract an awful lot of people for this to work. I caught her up. "How about we hide somewhere and come out later, when everyone has gone?" I said.

"*You* can," Jess said. "I've got training. I'm not missing it. If you want my help, you have to do this now."

I thought of Miss Smallbone, and how upset she'd be if she couldn't resurrect the dodo. This was *important*. I sped up and barged past Jess. "Over there," I said. "Blend with that pack of brownies."

I wouldn't say we blended well, but Brown Owl had very thick glasses and handed me an information sheet, so I think we got away with it. The sheet said the closest living relative to a dodo was a pigeon and they were hunted to extinction by sailors in 1668. It didn't mention Sidney "Squid-Hands" Smallbone or kumquats, though.

Brown Owl marched us past some life-sized dodo replicas. They were so cool with their great beaks and stumpy little legs. Imagine having a *dodo* as a pet? Maybe if there were any spare, Miss Smallbone would let me have one?

"There, George," Jess steered me towards a cabinet. I peered through the glass at a selection of brown and crumbly bones. Which would be the best to take?

"The wishbone's quite small?" Jess suggested.

I shook my head. "They might miss that. I'll take that tiny one there." I pointed to one by the beak.

Jess inspected the cabinet. "The door's around the back. You'll have to slide underneath. Pretend you've dropped something. I'll create the diversion, and when everyone's looking the other way, type in the combination."

"OK," I said. "How long do you think I'll have?"

Jess shrugged. "No idea. I haven't decided what I'll do yet. You'll have to gauge it."

How reassuring. I watched her walk off, then

"accidentally" dropped my information sheet. I'd just crouched down to pick it up when there was a massive crash.

It came from the entrance hall.

Normally I trusted Jess to do the right thing – but *that* had sounded worrying. Everyone else seemed to think so too. The place was in uproar. Attendants were running back and forth, the brownies were squealing and Brown Owl was trying to count them and push them towards the exit at the same time. I almost got up and ran after them, but then I remembered what I was there for.

This was it.

I threw myself under the cabinet and rolled to the back. There was the lock. I started typing in numbers. 19121960. Nope. 19121959. Nope. 19121961. There was a ping. YES! I pulled open the door, checked no one was looking and stuck my head in. I selected the tiniest of the tiny bones and gazed at it. I was holding a piece of dodo. How incredible was that?

I popped the piece of dodo in my pocket.

Time to go.

I closed the door and reset the lock, then slid out into the stampeding brownies. There was Jess! She was pushing her way towards me.

"What did you *do*?" I asked.

"Nothing." Jess grabbed my arm. "Come on, let's go."
She dragged me along.

"I got the bone," I said.

"Great." Jess didn't seem as excited as I thought she
should be. "Hurry up." She pulled me into the entrance
hall.

Eh? What on earth had happened? I blinked through
a haze of plaster dust. The Tyrannosaurus rex lay in a
heap. I turned to Jess. "Did—

I stopped as something large and hairy charged past
me, pursued by three museum attendants.

I stared after them. "Is that *Boris*?"

"Keep walking," Jess muttered. She marched me
towards the exit. "If anyone asks, we don't know him."

"We can't just *leave* him," I protested.

"We'll wait for him outside," Jess said.

TWENTY-FOUR

All the people standing outside on the National History Museum steps were making annoyed noises and wanting their money back. Brown Owl was *particularly* vocal. I shook my head. I couldn't *believe* Boris hadn't done what he was told and stayed put.

Animal training wasn't as easy as people made it out to be.

Jess and I skulked off and hid behind a potted palm. "He'll find his way out eventually," she said. "We'll grab him then."

We waited for ages but Boris didn't appear. Jess checked her watch. "We can't wait for ever," she said. "I'll have to go in. I'll say I was walking him for my gran, and he ran off."

"We haven't got a gran," I said.

"It *sounds* better," Jess said.

She had a point. "I'll come with you," I said.

Jess shook her head. "Stay here. You don't want to get caught with the bone."

I watched her walk back up the steps and into the museum.

Then I watched her being marched straight back out.

By Mr Mason.

Drat.

Should I run?

No, I couldn't leave her.

Jess pointed to the palm I was hiding behind. Hey! I stared indignantly. She'd grassed me up!!

I should have left while I had the chance.

We were in the museum office. Jess and I sat across the desk from a pink and furious Mr Mason. His shiny suit wasn't so shiny any more, as it was covered in plaster dust.

Boris looked sheepish in the corner.

A tiny bone lay in front of us, in a Ziploc bag.

I had a feeling we were in Really Bad Trouble.

Mr Mason ranted quite a lot. He said stealing from a museum was a terrible thing to do, and talked about calling the police. He said we'd have to come back in at the weekend and put the Tyrannosaurus rex back together. He said he'd be having a word with our mother, and made Jess write down our names and address. I hoped she might put our old address, but she didn't.

Mr Mason seemed surprised when he saw we lived at Hogweed Hall. He said he knew Dr Gupta, and that she used to work with him. Then he stared at us for a while. His face was less pink, which I felt was a good sign.

He looked at the Ziploc bag, and seemed to be thinking.

Finally, he spoke. "Tell me," he said. "Why a dodo bone?"

"It was because we lost Miss Smallbone's hat," I said.

"Miss Smallbone's hat?" Mr Mason leant forward.

I was so relieved he wasn't talking about the police any more I told him all about Miss Smallbone's project and Dr Gupta and the chickens and the dodo DNA, and how Jess had taken the hat to the charity shop. And then Jess explained how we'd got the hat *back* and I'd thrown it in the river. I was about to tell him about the flea, and that throwing the hat in the river hadn't been my fault, when he gave a snort.

Eh? I blinked at him. Was he *laughing*?

He *was*.

When he'd stopped, he gave a little clap. "So, Dr Gupta has perfected the technique, has she?" He smoothed his moustache. "She must be over the moon?"

"I think so," I said. "She doesn't know I know."

"I won't tell her." Mr Mason seemed quite jolly now. "It's about time she made a breakthrough. She's been working on it long enough."

"She hasn't hatched any dodos yet," I said. I pointed at the bone. "Which is why we needed that."

Mr Mason stood up. "I understand *why* you took it, but you can't go round helping yourself to exhibits." He walked round the desk. "Still, as I've got it back, we'll say no more about it."

"Really?" Jess breathed out in relief.

Mr Mason ushered us towards the door. "Can I ask you something?" he said.

"What?" I looked up at him.

"Don't mention me to Dr Gupta. We had a falling out."

Dr Gupta probably fell out with a lot of people. "What about?" I asked.

"I had to let her go." Mr Mason looked sheepish. "You know. Give her the sack."

"Why?" Jess asked.

"She wasn't always *trustworthy*, I'm afraid."

I blinked at him. "Wasn't she?"

He shook his head. "Sadly not. But I'm glad someone gave her the chance to carry on doing what she loved." He held the door open. "One last thing."

"What?" I said.

Mr Mason looked down at Boris. "Don't bring him here again, will you?"

"I don't think you should have done that," Jess whispered as we walked down the stairs from the office.

I looked at her. "Done what?"

"Told him about Miss Smallbone's project. Wasn't it supposed to be a secret?"

Oh. I blinked. Jess was right. Miss Smallbone had made me promise not to say, but I'd forgotten. "I don't think she'd *mind* him knowing," I said. "He seems nice enough." I paused. "Don't mention it to her anyway." I paused again. "Don't mention *you* know either."

Jess rolled her eyes. "You're such a blabbermouth, George. You're almost as bad as Muriel."

I scowled. "I'm jolly well not."

Boris pushed past me. He didn't look at all sorry for his part in this afternoon's disaster. "You better put your dog on his lead," I said. "In case he runs amok again."

"You were supposed to train him." Jess scowled at me. "What a waste of a day."

"*Actually*," I looked smug, "it wasn't."

"No?"

"No." I shook my head. "You know when Mr Mason asked for the bone?"

"Yes."

"I didn't give it to him."

"You didn't?" Jess blinked.

"No."

"What was in that Ziploc bag, then?"

I giggled. "One of Boris's bone treats."

Jess stared at me. "Where's the bone you stole?"

"In my other pocket." I held it up triumphantly.

That wasn't the *best* idea.

Boris saw the three-hundred-and-fifty-eight-year-old dodo bone in my hand and in one chomp it was gone.

We tried to prise his jaws open, but it was too late.

He'd swallowed it.

"We could wait a couple of days?" I suggested brightly. "See if it comes out?"

Jess looked at me.

I think that was a no.

TWENTY-FIVE

Jess took Boris for a run on the common while I went to explain things to Miss Smallbone. I didn't go into a lot of detail. I told her about the hat, but I didn't mention the museum, or that I'd told Mr Mason about her dodo project.

Even so, she wasn't impressed.

"Sorry," I said.

"I should hope you are," Miss Smallbone tutted. "I *liked* that hat. Luckily for *you*, there's a lot of feathers on a dodo. Twelve-Toe Tina didn't just make a hat and a fan – she made a lampshade too. The one in your mum's room."

The lampshade in Mum's room? There was a whole *lampshade's* worth of dodo feathers? I stared at her accusingly. If she'd mentioned that this morning, it would have saved a whole lot of trouble!

Miss Smallbone glowered back at me. "Don't worry. I won't be asking you to fetch it. I'll send Dr Gupta. She's less likely to give it away, or throw it in a fast-flowing river."

I scowled. There was no need for her to go on about it. I'd *said* I was sorry. I changed the subject. "What will you do with the dodos?" I asked. "When they're hatched. Give them to the zoo?"

Miss Smallbone gasped. "Absolutely *not*," she said.

"You're keeping them here?" I stared at her in excitement. That would be *brilliant*!

Miss Smallbone closed her eyes. "The whole *point*, George, is to return them to the island whence they came."

I stared at her. "The island?"

"Yes, George." Miss Smallbone gave me a friendly whack across the shoulders. "The island. What did you think? That I was going to raise them in the henhouse?"

The truth was, I *hadn't* thought. I double-checked before I allowed myself to panic. "By the island, you mean Hornswagg? Hornswagg Rock?"

"Of *course*, Hornswagg Rock. They'll be safe there.

158

It's uninhabited. Once I've settled the dodos, I shall use dynamite to blow up the bay." Miss Smallbone drew her plastic cutlass and brandished it in the air. "Neither ship nor charlatan will land again."

My voice came out in a squeak. "What about if it isn't uninhabited? What if someone is already on it?"

"Like *who*?" Miss Smallbone said. "No one would be able to sail through those rocks without a map. No. The dodos will be safe on Hornswagg, away from the evils of man." She shook her fist. "They will never again grace a blackheart's table."

A terrible vision of Muriel wielding a carving knife filled my mind.

"Not long now." Miss Smallbone threw back her head and gave a little twirl. "I will finally be free of *dodo à la kumquat*."

I stared at her. I needed to get that map back before Mildred and Muriel found it. "That's brilliant." I faked a smile. "Do you mind if I use the secret staircase? I've just remembered something I need to do."

Miss Smallbone twirled again. "Be my guest," she said.

I went past my room and down to Mildred and Muriel's. I listened at the panel for a moment, to make sure no one was in there, then quietly slid it back. The room was empty, so I stepped into it.

When I say empty, I mean empty.

No suitcases overflowing, no foot spa, no eye masks on the pillows. If it hadn't been for the untidy beds and a crumpled sheet of paper on the floor, you'd never have known Miss Smallbone's sisters had been there.

I picked the paper up and smoothed it out. My heart sank as I read it. Things were worse than I'd thought. I pulled open the wardrobe door, even though I knew what I'd find.

I was right. The dresses had gone, and so had the map. My plan had worked – but I'd ruined Miss Smallbone's.

Muriel and Mildred would dig and dig until they'd found that ruby. They'd wreck the island. It'd be no place for dodos.

I closed the wardrobe door and went and sat on Mildred's bed.

Why did I *never* think things through?

Why did I always mess things up?

Why was I so *rubbish*?

There was a sudden noise, and Jess stuck her head round the door. "Hi," she said. She looked around at the bare room. "They *have* gone, then? I thought I saw them drive off."

I didn't say anything.

"I thought you'd be pleased." She came in. "What's wrong? Was Miss Smallbone cross about the hat?"

I shook my head. "Not really. There's a load more DNA in Mum's lampshade."

"Why the misery, then?"

"The map to Hornswagg," I confessed. "I left it out for Mildred and Muriel to find."

Jess blinked "And that was a good idea *why* exactly?"

"I was worried they'd murder me." I stared dismally at the floor. "I thought if they had the map, they'd go and find the ruby and leave me alone." I gestured to the empty room. "And they have."

Jess shrugged. "It's not the end of the world," she said. "I bet the ruby's here. We haven't even had chance to start looking yet."

"You don't understand," I wailed. "It *is* the end of the world. Miss Smallbone was planning to settle the dodos on Hornswagg – and now Mildred and Muriel will be there, digging it up and ruining it."

"Oh." Jess sat down. "Well, you weren't to know. She should have told you at the start." She looked at me. "You can say it was me who left the map out, if you like?"

I shook my head. "It's OK."

"You worry too much," Jess said. "How much damage can two old ladies and a spade do?"

"They're not taking a spade," I said. I held out the paper I'd found on the floor. "They've hired a bulldozer."

TWENTY-SIX

We found Miss Smallbone in the kitchen. "Mildred and Millicent have gone out," she said. "If they come back, I'll nip down the stairs to the basement."

"I don't think they *are* coming back," I said.

Miss Smallbone looked thrilled. "You got rid of them?"

"They found the map," I said. "They've gone to Hornswagg to look for the Constantine Ruby. With a bulldozer."

Miss Smallbone roared with laughter. "You're so funny, George."

"It's not a joke," I said.

Miss Smallbone stopped laughing, though her mouth did carry on opening and closing for a while.

"Sorry," I said.

"But how did they find it?" Miss Smallbone was purple now. "I'd have moved it from their room, but it was inside one of Sidney's journals. Mildred and Muriel don't *read*. I couldn't have found a safer hiding place."

I mumbled something.

"Pardon?" Miss Smallbone looked at me.

I said it again, louder. "I MAY HAVE FOUND THE MAP AND LEFT IT OUT."

There was a silence.

I took advantage of it.

"I thought they might murder me," I explained. "I was worried. I didn't know you needed the island for the dodos. If I had, I'd never have done it."

"If you'd told George *everything*," Jess told Miss Smallbone off, "this would never have happened."

Miss Smallbone looked at Jess, then back at me. "George," she said. "Did you tell Jess about the dodos?"

"Sorry," I hung my head. "I forgot it was a secret."

Miss Smallbone sniffed. "I guess she's family. As long as you haven't told anyone else?"

I thought of Mr Mason. "Not a soul," I lied.

"That's something, I suppose." Miss Smallbone stood up. "There's only one thing for it," she said. "Come on."

We stared at her. "What?" I said.

"I'm bringing the plan forward. We need to get to the island before they do."

"I didn't think you had dodo eggs yet." Jess stared at her.

"We'll take the trial batch," Miss Smallbone said. "They'll be fine."

"They *know?*" Dr Gupta was purple. "George and Jess *know?*" She glared accusingly at Miss Smallbone. "We said this would be a secret between ourselves."

"I forgot myself," Miss Smallbone said. "Easy to do."

"That's right," I agreed wholeheartedly. "*Very* easy."

"I told George, and *he* told Jess," Miss Smallbone explained. "And *then* Mildred and Millicent got hold of a map and are on their way to Hornswagg as we speak."

"Mildred and Millicent? On their way to *Hornswagg?*" I thought Dr Gupta was going to faint.

"With a bulldozer." Miss Smallbone nodded.

"A *bulldozer?*" Dr Gupta collapsed on to a lab stool with a sob.

"There's no need to be so dramatic," Miss Smallbone tutted. "The long and short of it is, we need to get there before they do. Head them off." She pointed to the incubator. "We'll bring the plan forward and take the eggs we've got."

Dr Gupta shook her head. "You can't. I'm not convinced the feathers in that fan—"

"The feathers in that fan were *dodo*." Miss Smallbone glared at her. "They were *exactly* the same as the ones on my hat."

"I can't agree." Dr Gupta glared back at her. "But if you insist, I'll go and get your *dodo* eggs ready for you." She got up and stomped over to the tanks.

I stared after her. What had Mr Mason meant when he said she wasn't trustworthy? Did Miss Smallbone know? Maybe I should tell her? But if I did that, I'd also have to tell her about the National History Museum and the Tyrannosaurus rex and Boris eating the dodo bone, and we didn't really have time for lengthy explanations.

Jess put her phone away. "I've cancelled their bulldozer – *and* their boat. That should buy some time."

A crash from outside made me jump. "What was that?" I said.

Miss Smallbone peered through the window towards the fire escape. "Nothing to worry about. Looks a like plant pot toppled over. Must have been the wind."

I hadn't noticed any wind.

A shiver ran down my spine. Suppose there was someone out there?

Of *course* there wasn't. I gave myself a talking-to. I had no reason to worry. Mildred and Millicent had got what they wanted and gone. There wasn't anyone else who wanted to finish me off.

Miss Smallbone turned back to us. "Jess. If you and George pack a rucksack each, we can be at the airfield in an hour."

I stared at her. She was taking us? To Hornswagg?

Jess blinked. "I can't go anywhere," she said. "The championships are next week. I need to train."

Miss Smallbone blinked. "Jess. I don't think you understand. We're talking about the resurrection of the *dodo*—"

"I know *that*," Jess said. "It's just the—"

Miss Smallbone held up her hand. "If you don't want to come, Jess, then don't you worry one bit. It's not a problem. I could have done with the help, but you stay and do your swimming. After all, you can never have too many trophies."

"It's not about the trophies—" Jess began.

"George will come, won't you, George?" Miss

167

Smallbone walloped me on the back. "We'll make a brilliant team."

I jumped up. "What should I bring?"

Jess butted in. "Miss Smallbone, you can't take George to Hornswagg if I don't go."

My mouth fell open. I stared at her in horror. Was she *kidding*? This was my one chance to make a *difference*.

Miss Smallbone looked most put out. She glared at Jess. "Why can't I take him? I'm a responsible adult."

"You pretended to be *dead*," Jess said.

"For a very good reason." Miss Smallbone refused to be embarrassed.

"Well, you can't." Jess folded her arms. "He's only eleven. Mum wouldn't like it."

Mum probably wouldn't. But then again, Mum had asked two murderers to babysit, so she wasn't always a good judge of what was best for us.

Miss Smallbone scowled. "So, what you're *saying*," she huffed. "Is that either you *both* come, or *neither* of you come – and you're *refusing* to come, Jess, so you're spoiling it for poor George."

"I'm not *refusing*," Jess said. "It's—"

"So, you *will* come?" Miss Smallbone clapped her hands. "That's *wonderful* news."

"That's *not* what I said." Jess rolled her eyes.

"Gracious, you do keep changing your mind. Don't worry." Miss Smallbone pulled out her phone. "I'll leave both of you here. I shall telephone that lovely Mr Wickom and see if *he* would like to help."

My eyes felt scratchy. I couldn't imagine anything more brilliant than taking dodo eggs to a tropical island and waiting for them to hatch. And now I wasn't allowed.

Jess saw my face and wavered. "Do you *really* want to go, George?" she asked.

Yes, I did really want to go.

Badly.

But Jess had trained every day for a year and it wouldn't be fair if she lost the championship because of me. I sat back down. "It's OK," I told her. "I don't mind."

Jess went quiet.

"Honestly," I said. "It's fine."

Jess shook her head. "You know what, George? I think I'd *like* to go."

I blinked.

"I've won enough races. It doesn't matter if I come last this year." She turned to Miss Smallbone. "What do we need to pack?"

TWENTY-SEVEN

Miss Smallbone said we were going to Hornswagg by plane and that *she* would be flying us. Jess looked like she was going to change her mind when she heard that, but Miss Smallbone told her there was no need to worry, as she'd been flying for years and her plane was in excellent working order.

"It's not very big but it's extremely fast," she said.

"Will we land on Hornswagg?" I asked.

Miss Smallbone shook her head. "It's not big enough for a runway. We'll touch down on the mainland, then take my ship."

"You have a *ship*?" Jess said.

"Of course," Miss Smallbone said. "*The Windy Pig.* I got her out of storage a few weeks ago. I've told the harbour master we'll be setting sail as soon as we get there." She turned to Jess. "Have you packed for Boris?"

"We're taking Boris?" Jess looked surprised. "I didn't think there'd be room."

"There's always room for dear Boris." Miss Smallbone gave him a pat. "He can squidge in with you."

"Great," said Jess, not looking like she thought it was great at all.

"Dr Gupta? How are you getting along with the eggs?" Miss Smallbone bustled over to her. "I thought we'd put George in charge of those?"

Me?

"They're ready." Dr Gupta had wrapped each egg in bubble wrap and put them in a rucksack. She held it out. I eyed it nervously. How I was expected to carry a dozen eggs and not break them?

Dr Gupta rolled her eyes. "It's not *any* old rucksack," she said. "It's shock absorbent. The top has a solar panel in it, which charges the battery at the bottom." She pointed to it. "That runs heat through wires in the fabric and keeps the eggs at optimal temperature. All *you* have to do is carry it."

"OK." I took it.

"Check each egg daily, for signs of hatching. Ideally, they won't hatch until you're safely on Hornswagg."

"Right," I said.

"If they *do* hatch, feed them these." Dr Gupta handed me a bag. "Mealworms. After three days they eat regular worms. You'll have to dig for those."

"OK," I said. "I'll take a spade. Is that everything?"

"One last thing," Dr Gupta said. "When chicks hatch, they think the first thing they see is their mother. It's called imprinting." She handed me a picture of a dodo. "The second they pop their head out the shell, show them this. Don't forget."

I looked at her to see if she was joking, but she didn't seem to be, so I slipped the picture into the rucksack with the eggs and the mealworms.

"Good luck." Dr Gupta sounded almost civil. "I hope it works out. Miss Smallbone has put a lot into this project."

"I know," I said. "I'll try not to mess it up."

TWENTY-EIGHT

When Miss Smallbone had said the plane wasn't very big, she wasn't exaggerating. There were only three seats, one behind each other, and a glass dome above them that you lifted up to climb in, then pulled back down before take-off.

"As George is looking after the eggs, he needs the back seat. It's roomier," Miss Smallbone said. "Jess? You share the centre seat with Boris."

"How lovely." Jess clambered in and Boris squeezed himself next to her. He looked a lot more impressed with the arrangement than she did.

"There are parachutes under your seats." Miss Smallbone spun the propeller, then climbed into the front. "Put them on. It's not so easy if you wait until we plummet."

Jess pulled hers out and peered at it. "Mine's a bit moth-eaten," she said.

"They're fine," Miss Smallbone said. "They've all been checked."

"Are we likely to need them?" Jess buckled hers tightly.

"Of course not." Miss Smallbone guffawed. "These old planes are wonderfully reliable."

Jess didn't look convinced.

"If things *do* get tricky," Miss Smallbone went on, "push the button to the left of you. That's it. The red one. It will activate your ejector seat."

Jess looked pale. "Then what?"

"Pull that cord." Miss Smallbone pointed to the parachute. "And aim for somewhere soft."

I noticed a sheen on Jess's brow. She wasn't *nervous*, was she? Jess was *never* nervous.

"Is there a parachute for Boris?" she asked.

"Afraid not," Miss Smallbone said. "But don't worry, I'm not planning to crash. All set?"

Jess pushed Boris's hairy face away from hers and turned around to face me. "I just wanted to say goodbye, just in case. Also. I'm a bit hot with Boris here. If you fancy swapping places, just say."

I patted the rucksack in my lap. "I'm in charge of the eggs, otherwise I would have done," I lied. "I can't risk Boris squashing them."

Miss Smallbone pulled down the glass dome. It clicked into place.

There was no going back.

We started to trundle along the runway. It got bumpier and bumpier and then suddenly it wasn't bumpy any more. We were in the air. I watched the city get smaller and smaller.

Wow.

This was *brilliant*.

What *wasn't* brilliant was Boris's tail. It was sticking through the gap between the seat and the wall, and he kept twitching it. If he was a *small* dog, it wouldn't have mattered at all – but Boris's tail was as massive as the rest of him. It was quite annoying.

I pushed it back through the gap.

"Hang on to those eggs." Miss Smallbone bellowed above the engines. "We're heading for cloud. It'll be choppy."

As if to demonstrate, the plane gave a lurch and dropped several feet.

"Fun, isn't it?" Miss Smallbone chortled from the front.

A matter of opinion, I felt.

Jess was quiet. She seemed to have her eyes shut. I leant forward and tapped her on the shoulder. "Are you OK?" I asked.

"Nope."

"What's wrong?"

"I don't like heights."

"Don't you?" I stared at her in surprise. "I never knew."

"Nor did I." She opened one eye, then shut it again with a moan.

"We'll be fine," I said. "We've got parachutes."

"Wearing them reminds me there's a possibility we might have to use them," Jess hissed.

"It'll be night-time soon," I said. "Then you won't be able to see how high we are."

"That doesn't make me feel any better."

The plane lurched again. Jess buried her face in Boris.

"Shall we do a loop the loop?" Miss Smallbone called from the cockpit. "Before it's too dark to see?"

"Not right now," I called back. "Jess isn't feeling great."

"OK." Miss Smallbone pulled down her goggles. "Both of you should get some sleep. It's a long flight."

I checked the eggs were nice and warm in the rucksack, then covered myself with my coat and listened to the rush of the wind and the hum of the engines. The next thing I knew, something bright was shining and Jess was screaming.

TWENTY-NINE

The bright thing was the sun, and that was above us.

We were heading away from it.

This must be the plummeting Miss Smallbone had talked about.

"Nothing to worry about," Miss Smallbone shouted. "Just another air pocket."

An air pocket? It was a jolly *big* air pocket!

It was the final lurch that did it. I grabbed on to the rucksack with one hand and the seat with the other.

And *that* was the moment Boris's tail thumped back through the gap and hit my eject button.

The next few seconds were a blur. I was heading up for what seemed like ages. Then I was heading down. The hum of the plane faded into the distance.

It was ever so quiet.

Why couldn't I see anything?

Oh. My eyes were shut.

I opened them.

Blimey.

The ground was a long, *long* way beneath me. I still had hold of the rucksack. That was good, wasn't it? What now? I had to do something. Miss Smallbone had distinctly said ... I frowned ... what was it she'd said?

"Pull the cord, George. PULL THE CORD!!" Jess's voice came from above me.

The cord.

I groped around with the hand that wasn't holding the rucksack. Ah, there it was. I tugged as hard as I could and waited.

Was something supposed to happen? Nothing had. I tugged the cord again. Still nothing. I kept tugging. Then I started to panic. The ground was a long way off, but if my parachute didn't open soon, I'd—

"*George.*" Jess was beside me. She was clinging on to Boris – who looked surprised at the change of scene, despite it being his fault.

"I pulled the cord," I gabbled in terror. "It doesn't work."

"You're unravelling your jumper." She reached out with her free hand. "It's this one."

There was a jolt, and I shot up and up and up.

My parachute billowed above me.

Oh joy. It was nice being the right way round.

So nice.

I started breathing again.

I wasn't going to die.

I could see everything from here. Fields. Forests. Villages. Was that the sea? It *was*. It was so blue it blended into the sky. We'd been to Morecambe once. The sea wasn't that colour, let me tell you. I waited for Jess to bob up next to me, but she didn't.

I peered down. Why was she so far away?

Why was she getting *further* away?

Why was her parachute not open?

A moth flew past me.

A moth? Up here?

It felt like there was ice in the pit of my stomach.

Had moths destroyed her parachute?

I stared in horror as my sister spun below me. She had her arms wound tightly around Boris, as if he could save her.

Not Jess.

What would I tell Mum?

I couldn't watch any longer.

I screwed my eyes tight shut.

There was a rush of air. "George?" a voice bellowed in my ear. "Are you OK?"

Eh?

I opened one eye and then the other.

Oh.

Jess was drifting a few yards away. Her parachute was open and didn't have moth holes in it. Boris looked even more confused than he normally did.

"Are you all right?" she said.

"I'm fine," I said. "Perfectly fine."

"Why did you eject yourself?" she asked. "It was only an air pocket."

"I *didn't*." I scowled at her. "Boris hit the button with his tail." Then, because I'd sounded a bit rude, and she *had* just saved my life, I asked her how she was.

"I don't mind this. It's peaceful." She looked up. "There's Miss Smallbone's plane." She pointed at a dot high above us. "It's circling."

We were so busy looking up, the tree took us by surprise.

Boris yelped as we crashed through the branches. I

clung tight on to the rucksack as my parachute tangled and swung me into a fork in the trunk. It felt good to be safe.

Boris and Jess were dangling beneath me. I unstrapped my harness and pulled the rucksack on to my back. I peered through the leaves. "Are you OK?" I shouted.

"We're not far from the ground," Jess shouted back. "Can you cut through the cords?"

"What with?" I looked around frantically. "The penknife Mum won't let me have?"

"Anything. Hurry." Jess's voice rose in panic. "I can't hold Boris much longer."

"Hang on." I scrambled past them to the ground. "Drop him to me."

I realized what I'd said as I said it.

I looked up.

Boris's enormous hairy bottom swung gently above. It wasn't pretty, but I couldn't let him down. I took the rucksack back off and leant it carefully against a root. Then I braced myself. "Now," I shouted.

I didn't exactly *catch* him. More broke his fall.

He really was heavy.

"George?" Jess shouted down. *"George?"*

I wiggled out from underneath. "I'm OK."

"How about Boris?"

Boris was unperturbed. He was having a scratch. "He's OK too."

Jess unstrapped her harness and jumped down beside me.

"So," she said. "This is South Africa."

THIRTY

South Africa was *hot*. We took off our jumpers and gazed at acres and acres of yellow grass. "How come we managed to land in the only tree for miles?" I said.

"If anyone *asks*," Jess said, "say it was deliberate." She looked around. "This must be a plateau," she said. "Grazing land."

"I can't see any cows," I said.

"Not farm animals," Jess said. "Elephants and stuff."

I blinked at her. "You mean lions? Should we climb back up the tree?"

"They mainly hunt at night," Jess reassured me.

Mainly? I took a step back and pulled out my phone. "I'll ring Miss Smallbone."

"There's no signal," Jess said. "I've already checked. We'll have to walk."

Was she kidding? That grass was probably *full* of things waiting to pounce. Suppose a lion got Boris? There was quite a lot of meat on him. I looked at him lying by my feet. He had his head on his paws and looked ever so hot. I bent down to pat him.

Suddenly, he raised his head and barked. Then he jumped to his feet.

"What's he doing?" Jess grabbed his collar.

I scanned the horizon. Had he seen something? I hoped it wasn't anything that might eat us.

There *was* something. In the distance.

A dust cloud.

I pointed it out to Jess.

She peered through the haze. "It's coming this way." She took a step back. "What do you think it is? Wildebeest?"

I'd considered the risks of being *eaten*, but not trampled. "I think climbing back up the tree might be a good idea," I said.

"What about Boris?" Jess looked worried. "I'm not sure he's very agile."

It turned out not to matter what Jess thought of Boris's

agility. He had other ideas. He charged fast as he could towards the approaching dust, barking all the while.

"What's he doing?" Jess wailed. She shot after him.

"Jess!" I shouted. "No."

"I don't want him to get hurt," she called.

I stared after her. What was she thinking? Boris was a *dog*. He could dodge in and out of a million wildebeest hooves. Jess couldn't! I saw her grab him just before the dust closed around her. I had to get help. Maybe there'd be a mobile signal higher up the tree?

I grabbed the rucksack and ran. I scrambled up the trunk and into the lower branches as the dust curled up and made me cough. I couldn't see through it. Was I high enough? Wildebeest couldn't climb, could they? No. They were big and heavy and had hooves.

As I pulled out my phone, a thought struck me.

If wildebeest were big and heavy and had hooves, why could I not hear them? You'd think, wouldn't you, if a million wildebeest were stampeding towards me, there would be some noise? The ground might shake a bit?

The ground wasn't shaking. Not even a little.

There *was* a noise though, coming from the dust.

A low hum.

It didn't sound like wildebeest.

It sounded like an engine.

A car door slammed beneath me as the dust cleared a little. I peered down through the branches. "Oh," I said. "Hi."

Jess squinted up at me. "Miss Smallbone has come to collect us."

"Oh, right." I started to scramble down. "I wasn't scared, you know. I was just—"

"Hurry up," Miss Smallbone bellowed from the jeep below. "We're running out of time. At this rate the eggs will hatch on board."

I climbed into the back and held up the rucksack. "They're all fine."

"Thank goodness." Miss Smallbone slammed the jeep into reverse and shot backwards. "Hang on to them, it's bumpy."

She did a ten-million-point turn and finally we were facing the way she'd come. "Let's go."

"How did you find us so quickly?" I asked.

"There's a tracker in Boris's collar," Miss Smallbone said. "After you ejected, for no good reason—" She gave me a pointed look. "I landed as planned at the airfield. Then I borrowed this to fetch you in." She patted the side of the jeep.

"I'd like to say I only pressed my button because George pressed his," Jess said.

I glared at her. "I didn't press mine *actually*," I said. "Boris did."

"No need to squabble." Miss Smallbone took a corner on two wheels. "We need to get on. Mildred and Muriel's flight is due. If we don't get to the island before them, we're in trouble." She slammed her foot down, and after that I concentrated on hanging on.

THIRTY-ONE

I stood on the quay and blinked.

Partly to get the dust out of my eyes, but also in awe.

The Windy Pig. There she was.

She was a *proper* pirate ship. The rigging stretched high amidst great billowing sails. There was a real crow's nest – a half barrel attached to the mast, not a flat roof with a railing around it. On the deck at the back was a huge wooden wheel.

Miss Smallbone said it operated the rudder. "I'll show you in a bit. There isn't a Jolly Roger, I'm afraid. Moths got it."

"How long will it take to get to Hornswagg?" I asked.

"A couple of hours on a good day." Miss Smallbone peered at the sky. "Which it is."

Jess looked up from her phone. "That's not what it says here. It says squalls from eleven a.m."

"The forecast is always wrong," Miss Smallbone said. She licked her finger and stuck it in the air. "I trust my instincts."

Jess looked dubious.

"The sky *is* very blue," I reassured her.

"I guess."

Miss Smallbone rolled a keg towards the gangplank. I went to give her a hand.

"Careful," she said. "It's gunpowder."

I took a step back. "What for?"

"Cannons."

I blinked. "Are cannons allowed?" I asked.

"Absolutely." Miss Smallbone gave the keg a pat. "If we have to take my sisters out in self-defence, so be it."

"And what's that?" I pointed to something long under her arm.

"This?" She held it up. "It's a harpoon. Very useful at sea."

"What about your spud gun?"

She patted her britches. "Got that too. And a sack of King Edwards in the hold. Where's your sister?"

Jess was on the poop deck with Boris. She was staring

191

up at the crow's nest. "Don't ask me to go up there," she said. "I'll swab the decks, empty the sluice, splice the mainstays – *whatever*. But I'm all done with heights."

"I'll take your turn," I said. "Five pounds."

"Three," Jess said. "It's all I've got."

We were interrupted by a great clanking from underneath. "I've raised the anchor," Miss Smallbone shouted. "We're off."

The breeze filled the sails above me, and *The Windy Pig* started to move across the bay. I leant over the rail and watched the water race past. This was incredible. It didn't matter that I wasn't the best at anything. It didn't *matter* that my school report said AVERAGE. I was on a pirate ship with a rucksack full of dodo eggs.

I'd never be average again.

"George?" Miss Smallbone bellowed from the wheelhouse. "Where are you?"

"Coming," I said.

Miss Smallbone showed Jess and me how to work the rudder. She said if you spun the wheel left, the ship went right, and if you spun it right, the ship went left. But you didn't say left and right, you said *port* and *starboard*, and the wheel moved at a different speed to the rudder, so it was easy to get wrong.

As we zigzagged across the harbour, I thought Miss Smallbone was giving us a demonstration of how *not* to do it – but actually, she wasn't.

"You do know *how* to sail, don't you?" Jess asked.

Miss Smallbone looked nonchalant. "How hard can it be?" she said.

We stared at her. "But you're a *pirate*," I said.

"*Descended* from pirates." She corrected me. "Hogweed Hall is hardly by the sea. I never had chance to learn. Don't worry." She held up a book. "I have the instruction manual. I'm halfway through already."

We stood and looked at the approaching harbour wall. Jess reached out and adjusted the wheel. "Can I have a go?" she said. "I'd really like to."

"Wonderful idea." Miss Smallbone relinquished control.

"Shall I go up to the crow's nest?" I said. "Keep an eye out for Mildred and Muriel?"

"Yes," Miss Smallbone said. "There's a spyglass up there. Lash yourself to the mast. It could get choppy."

"OK," I said. I turned to go.

"Wait." Miss Smallbone called after me. "Give Jess the rucksack. The eggs will be safer down here."

I liked being in charge of the eggs, but I did as Miss

Smallbone said and handed them over. "Guard them with your life," I said.

Jess rolled her eyes. "OK, George," she said.

It wasn't easy climbing the rigging. Every time the ship hit a wave I almost fell off. I was exhausted by the time I got to the top. I sat in the bottom of the barrel to recover and then I picked up the spyglass and peered through it.

There was our dusty jeep, parked on the quay, and the harbour master napping in his deck chair. Apart from him, I couldn't see a soul. Everything was still. I swept the spyglass down to the other end and checked out the boats in the shallows. Most of them were small and wooden, but there was one that wasn't. A low, fast-looking speedboat with shiny red paintwork and chrome fittings. It was tethered a little closer to us than the others. I could just make out its name.

The Red Tornado.

It was nice, but I preferred *The Windy Pig.*

I checked back on the harbour master. Still asleep. I swept the spyglass back up the quay. Eh? *That* hadn't been there before.

There was a car parked next to the jeep. A big black one.

A wisp of smoke drifted from the exhaust.

Had Mildred and Muriel caught up with us already?

I kept the spyglass jammed to my eye until the car door opened and someone got out – but by then we were so far away all I could tell was that it wasn't either of Miss Smallbone's sisters.

Thank goodness for that.

THIRTY-TWO

"George?" Miss Smallbone shouted from the deck.

"What?"

"You're supposed to be looking out to sea."

"OK." I turned around and pointed the spyglass towards the horizon. "What am I looking for?"

"Things we might hit."

It was blowy now. *The Windy Pig* was racing through the water and it wasn't long before land was out of sight. I found a rope and tied myself to the mast, like Miss Smallbone had told me to. I squinted at the sky. It was darker than it had been. It looked like there was going to be a storm. I did hate it when Jess was right.

It didn't take long for the wind to change from a breeze to a gale. I tried to keep the spyglass to my eye, but the ship was pitching over enormous waves, so it wasn't easy. I scanned the horizon the best I could. Sea. Nothing but sea and spray and mist.

There was a rolling noise followed by a crash from below. One of the barrels must have broken loose. I hoped Jess and Miss Smallbone were all right. I shouted down to them over the wind, but they didn't reply.

I better go and check.

It was easier coming down the rigging than going up, but there were still some hairy moments. I felt safer on the deck even if it was lurching all over the place. I sidestepped a barrel and looked around for Jess and Miss Smallbone. I couldn't see them. I hoped they hadn't fallen overboard. It wasn't *that* choppy, was it?

I found Miss Smallbone first. She was leaning over the rail of the quarter deck. She was very green. "Are you all right?" I asked.

She motioned weakly with her hand. "Absolutely," she said.

"Are you seasick?" I asked.

"Don't be ridiculous." Miss Smallbone clung tight as the ship gave a great lurch. "I'm a pirate. I don't get seasick. The *very* idea." She draped herself further over the edge.

I waited politely. "Are you sure?" I said.

"It was something I ate," she croaked.

I helped Miss Smallbone below decks. She said she needed a lie-down.

When I came back up, I went to look for Jess. She was slumped against Boris in the wheelhouse.

"You're a funny colour," I said.

Jess closed her eyes. "I think I'm going to die."

"Should I take over?" I asked.

"It might be best." Jess struggled to her feet. "We're heading in the right direction. I put in the coordinates and locked the wheel off. You don't need to do anything."

"I'm supposed to be in the crow's nest," I said.

"I'll look out from the prow," Jess said. "If there's a problem, I'll send Boris back with a message." She staggered off.

I stared after her. Well, that was reassuring. Boris was *awful* at doing what he was told.

THIRTY-THREE

I hung on to the wheel as we ploughed through the waves. It was brilliant fun. Like a roller coaster, but with spray. I couldn't believe Miss Smallbone was seasick. *I'd* make a better pirate than her.

The sky wasn't quite as black now. Maybe the storm was passing? Even so, I should probably tie myself to something? I looked around. There was a bit of rope lying by the lobster pots. That'd do. I ran over and picked it up, then tied one end to the railing. I was about to tie the other around my waist when I saw something small, out at sea.

A fishing boat.

Its name was painted across the prow. *The Sea Biscuit.*

It was chugging through the spray towards us, and there were people in it.

Two people.

One was clinging on to her hat. The other had a spade tucked under her arm and was wrestling with the wheel. It was too late to duck out of sight. I stared at them, and they stared back.

Mildred and Muriel.

They looked surprised to see me.

Very surprised indeed.

None of us said anything for a while. Eventually I gave a cheery wave. "Hi there," I shouted. "Lovely to see you. What a coincidence."

Mildred shouted something back, but I couldn't hear her over the flapping sails. I cupped my ear to let her know.

She grabbed a megaphone and leant out of the cabin. "Why are you here?" she bellowed into it. "Did you follow us?"

"Of course not," I bellowed back. "Why would I do that? I'm on a fishing trip." I held up a lobster pot as evidence.

"Don't give me that." Mildred's hair was whipping about her face, and underneath it she was purple. "That's Sidney's ship. You're heading for Hornswagg."

"Horn what?" I pretended not to know what she was talking about.

"You're after the ruby." Mildred looked murderous. "Isn't it enough you inherited my house?"

"I'm not, and it wasn't your house," I said. "*Actually.*"

Mildred swung *The Sea Biscuit* alongside *The Windy Pig.* "Take the wheel, Muriel," she said. "Keep her steady. I'm boarding."

Boarding? Oh. I took a step back. I hadn't realized that was a possibility. I'd have been less rude.

"Give him what for, Mildred," Muriel squealed.

"I certainly will." Mildred readied herself to jump.

I looked down at her. It was a long way. I still didn't see how— Oh.

My *mistake* was not noticing the rope I'd tied to the rail had slipped down the side of *The Windy Pig.* Mildred was up it in seconds. She stood on the deck in front of me and brandished her spade. "You cancelled my bulldozer, didn't you? And our boat?" She pointed at *The Sea Biscuit.* "That was all they had left. It smells of squid."

"Sorry," I said. I took a step back and tripped over the lobster pot.

Mildred took a step forward. She stood above me, glowering. "Your mother said we could choose a memento."

"Yes, but—"

"Well, then." Mildred thumped her spade on the deck. "I choose the Constantine Ruby."

I wiggled back a bit. "I'm not sure the Constantine Ruby falls into the *memento* category," I said. "I was thinking a vase? There's lots of nice ones."

"Have you got him, Mildred?" Muriel scrambled over the rail and landed with a thud. "Shall we make him walk the plank?"

"We'll put him in the brig." Mildred looked around, then back at me. "Who are you here with?" she asked.

"No one." I got to my feet. "I'm here by myself."

"Rubbish." Mildred didn't believe me. She sent Muriel to check.

I hoped Jess had heard all the shouting, and had hidden. Muriel tottered back. "All clear," she said. "That awful dog is there, tied to the railing at the front, but no sign of anyone else."

That was good.

She looked at Mildred. "Shall I lock him up? The ruby-stealing weasel."

"I haven't stolen *anything*." I scowled at her. "I'm not even *interested* in the ruby."

"Of course you are," Mildred scoffed. "Who wouldn't be?"

"I'm not saying it wouldn't be *nice* to have a priceless jewel," I said. "But sometimes other things are more important."

Muriel looked thoughtful. "I mean, if you were *hungry* and it was a choice between the ruby and a doughnut—"

"Do be quiet, Muriel." Mildred stamped on her foot.

"Why do you even want it?" I asked. "You've got loads of money. You said so yourself."

"We are running a little low," Muriel confessed.

"It's not *about* the money, Muriel," Mildred snapped. "It's about what's *right*."

"What do you mean?" I asked.

"Mary was Father's favourite," Muriel explained. "She could do no wrong in his eyes."

"Oh?" I blinked.

"Yes." Muriel nodded. "She got the nicest things to wear, and the best toys – and there was the Christmas that— do you remember that Christmas, Mildred? Oooh, she was so mean."

Mildred nodded grimly.

"Mildred and I got tiddlywinks and Mary got a pony," Muriel went on. "She wouldn't even let us have a go."

"She said we could *brush* him." Mildred looked sour.

"Her curls were always perfect and she had a little button nose and everyone always looked at her and said, "Ooooh, *what a picture*." Muriel stamped her foot.

"Absolutely sickening." Mildred pretended to vomit.

"When Father told us about the ruby, Mary was desperate to find it. Thank goodness she didn't." Muriel closed her eyes. "The smugness would have been too much to bear."

"And after all that, he left her Hogweed Hall," Mildred spat.

Muriel placed a consoling hand on Mildred's arm. "After Martin ran away, Mildred always felt that as the eldest, Hogweed Hall should have been hers, by rights."

"And now *you* have it." Mildred glared at me. "The ruby is all that's left. You can't blame us for wanting it."

They stood there in front of me, festering.

"It doesn't sound like *any* of you were very nice to each other," I said. "Perhaps you should have tried harder?"

"Have you ever tried *living* with someone who's the favourite?" Mildred muttered. "It's very difficult."

"Actually." I glared back. "Jess is Mum's favourite, but I wouldn't *murder* her."

"Who said anything about *murder*," Mildred scoffed. "I can't say it didn't cross my mind, but—"

I stared at her. "You tried to murder Mary," I said. "I *know* you did."

"What rubbish," Mildred snorted. "I won't deny we forged a will. We'd read about Mary's near miss in the *Gazette*. It made us start thinking about Hogweed Hall, and who would inherit if she died."

"It awoke memories of the past." Muriel nodded. "The bitter resentment came bubbling back to the surface. Floated there like swill, it did."

"We *knew* she wouldn't leave Hogweed to us." Mildred scowled. "It wasn't *fair*. It should have been mine in the first place."

"It wasn't fair at *all*." Muriel patted her arm.

"We came up with a plan," Mildred said. "We forged a will leaving everything to us."

Muriel nodded. "I waited until she went out – then snuck in and hid it in her desk. It was *such* a good plan."

"And then she died," Mildred said. "Pouff." She flung her hands in the air. "*Just* like that. Such a coincidence. We realized at the memorial that Mary must have found the forgery and replaced it. We were *devastated*."

"You left out the bit about putting rat poison in her crumble," I said.

"We absolutely did *not* put rat poison in her crumble," Mildred snapped. "Murder our own sister? Muriel? Tell him we would *never* do such a thing."

Muriel gazed up at the sky. "I do declare the storm has cleared up," she said. "See? A patch of blue." She pointed. "Just over there. How lovely. Should we get going? The sooner we get to Hornswagg, the better."

"Muriel?" Mildred glowered at her.

Muriel hung her head. "I didn't mean to," she mumbled.

"Mean to *what*?"

Muriel burst into noisy sobs. "It was an *accident*. I'd put the will in her desk like we agreed, then I turned around and that awful dog was there. He chased me into the pantry and I climbed up on the shelf to escape him. I knelt on the squeezy ketchup – which gave me a bit of a shock – and that's when it happened."

"What?"

"I tipped a box of rat poison over. It spilled on to the crumble. I thought I'd scraped it all off."

207

Mildred stared at her. "Rat poison? In the crumble?"

"I distracted the dog with a sausage. While he was eating it, I managed to escape." Muriel dabbed her eye. "Then we got the letter from Mr Wickom about the memorial. I've not had a wink of sleep since. Every time I shut my eyes, I imagine she's in the room, clanking her chains."

"I can't *believe* you murdered Mary." Mildred looked furious.

"I knew you'd be cross," Muriel howled. "That's why I didn't tell you—"

She stopped, mid-sentence. Her mouth was still open, but the only thing that came out was a choking sound.

She pointed a shaking finger towards the main deck.

"What?" Mildred's head snapped round to look.

The colour drained from her face.

She swallowed.

"*Mary?*" she said.

THIRTY-FOUR

Miss Smallbone was staggering towards us. The voluminous Victorian nightdress she was wearing did nothing for her already green complexion.

What with the sea mist, and the spray, and the fact they thought they'd murdered her, I could *absolutely see* why Mildred and Muriel thought their sister was a ghost.

With terrible cries, they threw themselves over the side and into the sea.

"Who were you talking to?" Miss Smallbone said. "I thought I heard voices."

I pointed.

Miss Smallbone leant over the rail and watched her sisters thrashing about in the water. "We better get them

209

out," she said. "I'm not sure they can swim." She reached for a boat hook.

"I'm so sorry, Mary," Muriel wept. "I didn't mean to kill you."

Miss Smallbone smiled sweetly at Mildred. "Are you sorry, too?"

"The murdering was nothing to do with me," Mildred screeched. She tried to doggy-paddle away. "It was Muriel."

"What about forging the will?"

"Oh." Mildred stopped thrashing. "Yes, that was my idea."

"That doesn't sound like an apology." Miss Smallbone sniffed. "I think I'll leave you to the sharks."

"OF COURSE I'M SORRY." Mildred squawked in panic. "We behaved very badly. Now please go away. Go back to wherever ghosts live so we can get back on board."

Miss Smallbone looked at me. "Would you like to tell them, George?"

I stepped forward. "I'd love to," I said.

Once Mildred and Muriel were over the shock of their sister not being dead, she threw them a rope.

"George," Miss Smallbone called. "Can you give me a hand? I don't mean to be rude, but Muriel's a little heavier than she used to be."

"It *is* hard to keep the weight off in middle age," Muriel agreed as she scrambled over the railing.

"And you are quite fond of pie." Mildred climbed after her.

The three of them stood on the deck looking at each other.

Awkward.

Suddenly, Muriel flung herself at Miss Smallbone with a wail. "Can you forgive me?" she howled. "I was so jealous of your button nose."

"I think we should put everything behind us." Miss Smallbone patted her on the back. "A fresh start."

"How lovely." Mildred joined in the hug, though less enthusiastically. "We'll go to Hornswagg and search for the ruby together," she said.

"Actually," Miss Smallbone said, "we're not going to Hornswagg for the ruby."

"You're not?" Mildred blinked. "Why else would you be going?"

"We've got some eggs with us," Miss Smallbone said. "We're going to hatch them out in their natural habitat."

211

"Gracious." Muriel clapped her hands. "You've become a conservationist. How surprising! How *wonderful*! Will you allow us to help?"

"How very kind of you," Miss Smallbone said. "In actual fact, I do need some help – but you must say *no* if it's not your cup of tea."

Muriel linked her arm through Miss Smallbone's. "Ask away," she said.

"Once the eggs have hatched, I have to take George and Jess straight home. I need someone to keep an eye on the chicks for a week or so – until I get back, at least."

"What would we have to do?" Muriel asked.

"Nothing taxing," Miss Smallbone said. "Dig up a few worms. That's about it."

"Dig? You want us to dig?" Mildred looked delighted. "And if, while digging for worms, we should come across the ruby..." She beamed at Miss Smallbone. "You'll remember what Father said? Finders Keepers?"

"He *did* say that, didn't he?" Miss Smallbone beamed back.

I let out a sigh of relief. Thank goodness. No one was a murderer, and they were all friends again.

"Where *are* the eggs, George?" Miss Smallbone looked over.

"Jess still has them," I said. "She's on the front deck."

"She wasn't when I looked earlier." Muriel said.

Eh? Where was she then? "I'll go and check," I said.

"I'll come." Miss Smallbone followed me to the prow. Boris was there, tied to the railing and staring out to sea – but Jess wasn't. We checked under some barrels and an old tarp, but there was no sign of her

"She's swum off with the eggs!" Miss Smallbone shrieked. "She kept talking about that race suit she wanted. She'll sell them and use the money to buy one."

My mouth fell open. "Jess would *never* do that," I said.

"Wouldn't she? Sorry." Miss Smallbone apologized. "I forget not everyone's sisters are like mine."

"Where is she?" I said. "Did she go below?"

"Not while I was there," Miss Smallbone said. "I hope the eggs are safe."

I stared at her. "I'm more worried about Jess, *actually*," I said.

"There's not many places she can be." Miss Smallbone peered into a keg. "How about the crow's nest? Would she have gone up there?"

I shook my head. "No. She hates heights."

Mildred and Muriel clattered up behind us. "How wonderful that the sun's come out," Mildred said. "I was rather chilly in these wet clothes." She wrung her hat on to the deck.

"We can't find Jess," I said.

"Can't you?" Muriel wafted herself with her hand. "I'm sure she'll turn up. It's hot, isn't it? We might pick up a tan, Mildred."

Mildred didn't seem worried about Jess either. She trotted to the rail and peered over it. "Is that Hornswagg?" she said.

Miss Smallbone gasped and rushed to join her sister. "Already?" she said. "Gracious. I do believe you're right."

Hornswagg. We'd made it.

The rocks around it looked vicious, but beyond those were white sand and palm trees.

It was beautiful.

If only Jess would turn up.

THIRTY-FIVE

The sea was calmer now, so I went to untie Boris. If Jess was on this ship, he'd find her.

He was still sitting there, staring out to sea.

What was he looking at? I peered in the same direction.

Was that something? A speck in the distance? Whatever it was, it was getting smaller.

I turned and ran.

I ran past Miss Smallbone and Mildred and Muriel and swung myself up on to the rigging. Hand over fist, I pulled myself up into the crow's nest and grabbed the spyglass. I put it to my eye.

The speck came into focus.

It was *The Red Tornado*. The red speedboat I'd last

seen tethered at the quay. It was heading away from us, fast.

"Miss Smallbone?" I shouted down. "Can we speed up?"

"I expect so," she shouted back. There was a pause. "The book says we need to change the angle of the sails to catch more wind."

"We need to hurry." I stuck the spyglass in my pocket and started back down the rigging. "Jess has been kidnapped."

"Why would anyone want to kidnap Jess?" Miss Smallbone sounded puzzled.

I landed on the deck in front of her. "I don't know."

Mrs Smallbone stared out to sea, then gave a screech. "THE EGGS. JESS HAD THE EGGS!" She grabbed a rope. "Mildred? Muriel? I need some help."

I watched them scurrying about the deck. It didn't look like any of them knew what they were doing, but at last there was a groan and the huge sails swung around to catch the wind.

That was more like it.

The Windy Pig sped through the water like an arrow. I peered through the spyglass. We were catching up! We were close enough to see who was in the boat. There was Jess, looking furious in the back – and someone in the front, hunched over the wheel.

Who was it? Who even *knew* we had dodo eggs?

As I watched the hunched figure turned.

I almost dropped the spyglass.

It was Mr Mason, from the Natural History Museum.

"Mr Mason? That good-for-nothing old toad?" Miss Smallbone shrieked. "How could he possibly know what we were up to?"

"I have absolutely no idea," I lied.

She stamped her foot. "He's been snooping around since Dr Gupta stopped working for him."

I stared at her. "He didn't sack her?"

"Absolutely not. She left the day she discovered his plan."

"His plan?"

Miss Smallbone closed her eyes. "I can hardly say the words."

"Please do," I said.

"It wasn't just me who wanted to resurrect the dodo. Mr Mason did too. He hired Dr Gupta for her previous work cloning sheep. She thought they were a team, working towards the same scientific cause.

Then she discovered *this* on his desk." Miss Smallbone whipped a folded piece of paper from her pocket and handed it to me.

I opened it out. It was a flyer in festive colours.

TIRED of TURKEY?
LOST YOUR LUST FOR LEFTOVERS?
SICK OF SANDY SANDWICHES?
SUFFER NO MORE!
BE DIFFERENT
BUY DELICIOUS
BUY DODO
£5000 per bird

I blinked. "He wants to breed dodos for people to *eat*?"

"Yes." Miss Smallbone was puce. "An alternative to turkey. He's even built a factory. Dodo for the masses. He's planning to make a fortune."

"That's *awful*," I said.

Miss Smallbone nodded. "I knew he'd stop at nothing. He's a dangerous man."

I remembered the shadowy figure on the fire escape, and the noise at the attic window, and I stared out after Jess.

"Can we go any faster?" I said.

THIRTY-SIX

"How are we doing?" Miss Smallbone shouted.

I held the spyglass to my eye. "We're gaining," I said. "He's seen we're after him, but I don't think he can go any faster."

Miss Smallbone looked towards her sisters, who were sunning themselves on the deck. "Mildred?"

"Yes, Mary, dear?" Mildred sat up.

"Would you mind getting below and manning the cannon?"

"You can't use the cannon!" I turned to Miss Smallbone in horror. "Jess is in the boat!"

"Don't worry." Miss Smallbone reassured me. "We won't fire while the eggs are aboard."

Mildred looked disappointed. "Not even a warning shot?"

"Maybe one – but not until you hear me give the order."

Mildred saluted. She picked up her skirts and trotted off to the gun deck.

I sat on a crate and looked through the spyglass again. We were catching up! Mr Mason might have *The Red Tornado*, but *The Windy Pig* was faster.

Then, with a crunch, we stopped dead.

I went hurtling across the deck.

OW.

I extracted myself from a pile of dried cod, which had spilled from one of the barrels. "What happened?"

"Sandbank," said Miss Smallbone, furiously. "We've run aground."

"My hat!" Muriel ran to the side and gazed mournfully into the sea.

I stared after *The Red Tornado*. We'd never catch them now. We'd lost the eggs *and* Jess. What was I going to tell Mum?

Miss Smallbone looked as miserable as I felt. She patted my shoulder. "Don't worry, George. It was the eggs he wanted. He'll leave your sister at the harbour, I expect."

He'd better, or I'd have some explaining to do.

"Oh." Miss Smallbone peered out to sea. "How odd."

"What is?" I brushed off a bit of fish and stood up.

"They've slowed down."

"No." I grabbed the spyglass for a better look. She was right! They *had* slowed down – and turned around. They were heading straight for us! "What's he doing?" I said.

Miss Smallbone scowled. "He's seen we're stuck," she said. "The weasel's coming to gloat."

She was right. Mr Mason roared past *The Windy Pig* with a cheery wave. He circled twice, then cut his engine so he bobbed alongside us.

"Afternoon," he called up. "Not in trouble, are you? Can I help?"

"You dirty, dodo-stealing scoundrel," Miss Smallbone screeched. "Give my eggs back."

"I don't think I will." Mr Mason smirked. "Sorry."

Jess shouted from behind him. "I said if he took the eggs, he'd have to take me too. I'd swim for it – but I'm tied to the bench."

Boris stood on his hind legs and looked down at her. He barked, then gazed reproachfully at me, like her being kidnapped was my fault!

222

Maybe it *was*. I'd told her to guard the eggs with her life, hadn't I?

I needed to do something.

"Where's your spud gun?" I asked Miss Smallbone.

"All the weapons are downstairs," she said. "He'll be gone by the time I get back."

"Sorry to bother you." Muriel tottered over to the rail and leant over. "Could I trouble you to pass up my hat? It's just there." She pointed at it, floating in the water.

"This one?" Mr Mason fished it out and held it up.

"That's it." Muriel gave him a coquettish smile. "It's my favourite." She turned to Miss Smallbone. "Mary, dear, where's that stick thing you had earlier?"

Miss Smallbone handed her the boat hook. "Here you are."

"Thank you." Muriel lowered it over the edge. "If you could just pop my hat on this," she called. "That would be so kind of you."

Mr Mason stood up and leant toward the hook.

I held my breath. She was going to get him with it, wasn't she? She'd drag him out the boat and teach him a lesson! Who would have thought she'd have it in her! Well *done*, Muriel.

Muriel pulled the pole back up. It had her hat on it.

223

"Thank you so much," she cried. "I just love this hat. I'd have been so sad to have lost it."

I stared in disbelief. Yes. Very well done, Muriel.

"My pleasure." Mr Mason doffed his cap. "Now, I really must get going. So *lovely* to see you all again. Do take care." He slammed the throttle back and shot off in a cloud of spray.

I stared after them. I should have thought of a way to stop him. Why was I so useless? I slumped back down on the crate.

"Shall I fire the warning shot?" I heard Mildred's voice from below. She sounded keen.

"Not yet," Miss Smallbone said. "Wait for my signal." Then she said, "Why has he stopped?"

I looked where she was looking.

The Red Tornado was bobbing about on the waves. It was quite a long way off, but I could see Mr Mason was standing up. Was he stamping his foot? He was certainly shaking his fist.

"Do you know what, I think he's run out of petrol," Miss Smallbone snatched the spyglass from me and held it to her eye. "He's gone below. He must have more fuel down there."

This was my chance.

The boat couldn't be more than 200 metres away.

I had my 200-metre badge!

If I could get there before Mr Mason came back up, I could untie Jess and we could both swim to safety.

I climbed on to the rail.

"George?" Miss Smallbone's head snapped round. "What are you doing?"

I jumped.

The water wasn't cold, but it was very salty. It went up my nose and into my eyes. For a moment I thought I might change my mind and ask Miss Smallbone to fish me out with the boat hook, but I didn't. I threw myself forward and struck out for the shiny red speedboat.

THIRTY-SEVEN

Swimming in the sea wasn't like swimming in a pool. Not one bit. The waves kept slapping me in the face and my eyes were stinging and my arms got tired, but I kept going. I put my head down and ploughed through the water and didn't look up to see how far I had to go.

After ages, I decided I must be almost there by now and opened my eyes.

I wasn't.

I didn't seem to be any nearer to Mr Mason's boat at all.

But when I turned around and looked at *The Windy Pig*, it was miles away.

Miss Smallbone looked tiny on the deck. She waved at me, and I waved back, to let her know everything was fine. Then I started swimming again, but my arms really hurt, and I seemed to be lower in the water than before.

I hoped I wasn't going to drown. That'd be embarrassing.

Maybe a change of stroke?

I switched to doggy paddle and made a small amount of progress, when something brushed against my foot.

A shark?

I looked down at a great dark shape below.

I froze in terror.

That wasn't the best idea, as I sank.

To counteract the sinking, I started thrashing. *That* was about as good an idea as the last one.

It attracted the shark's attention.

I watched as he came up beneath me and then I squeezed my eyes tight shut and waited to be bitten in half, trying not to think about how much Mum would miss me.

Funny, though. I'd have imagined shark skin to feel like sandpaper – but this one felt . . . woolly?

Oh.

It wasn't a shark.

It was Boris.

Boris.

Lovely Boris.

I was on his back with my arms around his neck.

He'd saved my life.

He was really good at swimming. *Proper* doggy paddle. We got to *The Red Tornado* in no time – and Mr Mason was still below deck.

Boris paddled alongside while I reached for the edge. It was higher than I thought. I'd have to stand.

I knelt first to get my balance, then pushed myself up and grabbed the side. I slung myself into the boat and landed in a heap next to Jess.

She blinked at me. "You didn't swim all the way here?" She looked astonished.

"Yep," I said. I didn't mention I'd nearly drowned. "Boris helped a bit at the end." I undid the rope. "Take the eggs to the island. If you sit on Boris's back, they won't get wet."

"I'm not leaving you here," Jess said.

I glared at her. "I'm not a baby, Jess. Just go."

Jess shook her head. "The eggs are your thing." She shoved the rucksack into my arms. "You go with Boris, I'll follow."

There wasn't time to argue. I pulled on the backpack just as Mr Mason reappeared on deck with a petrol can.

When he saw me, his mouth dropped open. He stood and gaped for a moment, and then went purple and wanted to know how I got there.

"I swam," I said.

I wasn't going to tell him Boris was bobbing alongside the boat.

"Did you now?" Mr Mason suddenly smirked. "And what are you going to do now you've got what you came for? Jump overboard?"

"Maybe," I said.

"No, you won't." He gave a little giggle. "Because then the eggs will get wet and cold and none of them will hatch."

I tried to remember if Dr Gupta had said the rucksack was waterproof. It better be.

"I'll do you a deal." Mr Mason held out his hand. "Give me the eggs and I'll drop you on the island. It's no trouble."

"I'm not giving you the eggs," I said. "You want them for your dodo factory."

He looked surprised. "How do you know about that? I haven't told anyone yet."

I didn't want to get Dr Gupta into trouble. "I took a leaflet from your office," I said. "It was on the floor."

229

He shrugged. "No matter. I'm doing the world a favour. Everyone's sick of turkey. Soon, they'll be able to order a delicious dodo instead." He rubbed his hands. "Perhaps you'd like to join forces? There'll be SO much money in it."

"I'm not sure Miss Smallbone would be very happy," I said.

"That interfering old boot?" Mr Mason scowled. "I should have finished her off when I had the chance."

Jess stared at him. "You pushed the stone off the wall?!"

"I wanted to scare her. She shouldn't have poached my top scientist." Mr Mason started edging down the boat towards us. "Now give me those eggs, will you?"

"No," I said. "They're not yours."

"Yes, they *are*," Mr Mason said. "You got the dodo DNA from my museum. Don't think I didn't notice you'd swapped the stolen bone for a dog treat. I *let* you take it. It was the perfect solution. Dr Gupta would use it to create the dodo eggs, then I'd steal them. I had no idea you were planning on bringing them all the way here. I only discovered that yesterday, when listening at your kitchen window."

230

"Boris ate the dodo bone," I said. "Dr Gupta used the DNA from something else."

"Whatever." Mr Mason yawned. "I'm still keeping the eggs."

Jess looked at me. She gave me the tiniest of nods, then she stood up. "I'm off, if you don't mind?" she said. She climbed up on to the back of the boat, then plunged into the water.

Mr Mason looked rather surprised.

I stepped up on to the bench.

"You wouldn't dare." Mr Mason sniggered. "Think of the eggs."

"I am," I said. "Goodbye."

I stepped over the side.

THIRTY-EIGHT

"Go, Boris." I clung on to his back. "As fast as you can."

He didn't need telling. He set off after Jess. I looked over my shoulder. Mr Mason was staring after me, his mouth opening and shutting like a fish.

I gave him a wave.

That did it. He sprang into action. He dashed over to the fuel tank and started unscrewing the cap.

We wouldn't have long. Which way should I point Boris? Should we head for *The Windy Pig*? That would be safest. But the island was closer, and that was the way Jess had gone.

I heard Miss Smallbone shout something.

I couldn't hear the first time, over the wind and the waves.

But then she shouted it again.

And again.

It sounded like *shark*.

SHARK?

I looked around frantically.

Oh no.

Oh no no no no no.

A fin was cutting through the water towards us.

Even I could tell it was swimming ten times faster than Boris could.

There was no way to escape.

We were done for.

I looked on the bright side. At least if the shark filled up on me and Boris, it probably wouldn't manage Jess as well.

That was something.

I closed my eyes and waited.

Over the roar of the wind, I heard Miss Smallbone shout again. This time, she didn't say "SHARK." It sounded more like "MAKE READY."

And then she shouted, "FIRE!"

There was an explosion and a woosh, followed by a great slap as something hit the water.

I clung on to Boris as we were pounded by a massive wave.

Mildred had fired the cannon.

I looked behind again.

The fin was heading out to sea.

I let out a sob.

We were safe.

Only for a moment, though. We weren't far from Mr Mason's boat. The wave had knocked him off his feet, but he scrambled straight back up. I watched as he unscrewed the lid of the petrol can and began to fill the tank.

I turned towards the island. Through a gap in the

rocks I caught a glimpse of the beach lined with palm trees. "Go, Boris, *go*," I said. "It's not far. Look, see?" I leant forward and pointed.

Behind us, Mr Mason's boat roared into life. What would he do? Drive by and snatch the eggs? I turned to see.

It looked like that was exactly what he was planning.

I looked in desperation towards *The Windy Pig*. Miss Smallbone was still on the deck. She was aiming something in our direction. What was it? The spud gun? That wasn't going to be a lot of use!

There was a crack and a flash and something long and thin flew through the air at a million miles an hour.

She hadn't fired the spud gun.

She'd launched the harpoon.

It smashed straight through the stern of *The Red Tornado* just as it accelerated. The wire pulled taut, and Mr Mason's flashy red speedboat stopped dead.

Mr Mason somersaulted out and over our heads. He landed in the water with a huge splash.

The jolt had pulled *The Windy Pig* clean off the sandbank. Miss Smallbone and Muriel were cheering on the deck.

"Get the bad man," Muriel squawked. "Run him over. Let's have his guts for garters."

I grabbed the rope they lowered and they hauled Boris and me on to the deck. I pulled off the rucksack. "I don't think any have hatched yet," I said. "There's been no tweeting."

"Wonderful." Miss Smallbone looked mighty pleased. "We'll have time to build them a nest."

I looked out across the waves. "Did anyone see what happened to Jess?" I asked. "You don't think the shark came back, do you?"

"Oh no," said Muriel warmly. "Not the shark. You'd have seen the thrashing and all the blood. I suppose she could have been dashed to pieces on the rocks?"

"I expect she's waiting for us on Hornswagg," Miss Smallbone said. "Doesn't it look lovely?"

It *did* look lovely, but I still felt worried.

What if something terrible had happened?

I hoped it hadn't.

Miss Smallbone and Mildred hauled Mr Mason out of the water and on to the deck. He wasn't very happy. I'd learnt some good words from Miss Smallbone, but now I knew some even better ones.

"I'll put him in the brig." Mildred had him in a

headlock. "We'll decide how to dispose of him later."

She marched him off.

The wind had whipped up the waves again. I got the spyglass and peered through it. If Jess *had* made it to the island, why wasn't she standing on it waving at us?

"Do you think she drowned?" Muriel chirped. "Like Martin did?"

"No," I said. "She's a champion swimmer. She can't have done."

Mildred gave me a sympathetic smile. "You can have all the trophies in the world," she said. "But they're no use to you when you're caught in a current."

"Thanks." I glared at her. "Good to know."

Miss Smallbone dropped the anchor a little way out. "We'll wade in," she said.

I swung down the side of *The Windy Pig* and landed in the shallows. The water was warm and clear and full of tiny darting fish. I splashed through waves on to hot white sand and stared up at the mango grove beyond.

No Jess.

I blinked hard.

"What's wrong?" Miss Smallbone marched towards me.

"She's not here."

"Dangerous business, pirating." Muriel fanned herself with her hat. "That's why Father gave it up. If you don't get your throat slit in a skirmish then you feed the fish."

"Jess hasn't drowned." I scowled at her.

"If she *has*, at least she died doing something she loved." Muriel gave me a consoling pat.

"Thanks."

"Happy to help." She saluted. "I don't suppose you've got any snacks, have you?"

"No," I said. "I haven't." How could she even *think* of eating when Jess was still missing.

"Shall we check the eggs, George?" Miss Smallbone said. She held out the rucksack. "See how they're getting along?"

I shook my head. "You do it," I said.

"I'll help," Jess said, sitting down beside me.

THIRTY-NINE

Jess said she'd gone to look at the mango grove and got lost. "I only went a little way in. It all started to look the same. I had to climb a palm tree. I saw *The Windy Pig* in the bay so then I knew which way to go." She looked at Mildred and Muriel. "I must say I'm surprised to see you two here."

"They're friends now," I said. "Sort of."

"George thought you were dead," Muriel chirped. "He's such a gloombag."

I scowled at her. "I knew she'd be fine," I lied.

"It was harder than I thought," Jess said. "I should have stuck with you and Boris. I overestimated my abilities."

"Really?" I blinked. I wasn't sure Jess had ever done that before.

She nodded. "I had to swim against the current. For a while I didn't think I was going to make it."

"But you *did*."

"I remembered to focus," Jess said. "I pretended I was at the Olympics and Alice West was in the lead. That did the trick. I absolutely thrashed her." She lay back on the sand. "It's nice to be safe," she said.

"I don't want to interrupt the reunion." Miss Smallbone interrupted anyway. "George?" She held out the rucksack.

I carefully lifted each egg out and placed them gently on the sand. Jess helped me unpeel the bubble wrap.

Every one of them was perfect.

"Not a single crack." Miss Smallbone gave me a huge hug. "Well done."

"Yes, well done, George," Jess said.

"Thanks," I said.

Miss Smallbone pointed to the mango grove. "We'll build a nest up there. Under that fern. They'll need a bit of shade."

"Should I start digging for the ru— I mean, worms?" Mildred looked eager. "I've brought the spade."

"That would be marvellous," Miss Smallbone said. "Thank you."

Muriel jumped up. "I'll help. Perhaps we could start in the mango grove? I do like a nice ripe mango."

"Come on." Jess scrambled to her feet. "We're going to be part of history, George."

We carefully arranged a whole load of twigs and leaves, then laid the eggs inside.

"We'll take it in turns to watch them," Miss Smallbone said. "George? Do you want to take the first shift? It could be a long night."

I didn't mind. I got out the mealworms and made myself comfortable.

Jess and Miss Smallbone went to explore. They discovered the shack that Sidney Smallbone had built in 1668. "It'll be *perfect* for Mildred and Muriel to camp out in," Miss Smallbone said.

I wasn't sure it *would*. In my experience they liked electricity and running water and little plates of biscuits by the bed.

Mr Mason was allowed out of the brig to fix *The Red Tornado*. Miss Smallbone said she'd take Jess and me back to the mainland in it. She seemed to prefer it to *The Windy Pig*. "It's got a push button start," she cried. "And a proper steering wheel. So *easy*!"

Jess said, politely, that, as we weren't in a rush, she'd

prefer not to fly back home in Miss Smallbone's plane, and she didn't care if it took all her savings, but could she have a regular ticket?

Miss Smallbone looked hurt. "You don't get a parachute with the other airlines," she said.

"I'm OK with that," Jess said.

I sat next to the nest and looked over the sparkling sand to the bright blue sea. I'd never felt so at home *anywhere*. School seemed a world away. Maybe I could stay here? No. I'd miss Mum and Jess – and school wasn't *that* bad, and anyway, I couldn't wait to tell Tommy everything. I wondered if he'd believe any of—

Was that a tap? I stared at the eggs.

It *was*!

I needed to call Jess and Miss Smallbone! I scanned the beach. Where were they? The tapping got louder. I turned back to look.

Oh my.

From a pile of shell, a tiny chick struggled to its feet and glared at me at me with angry yellow eyes.

I couldn't breathe.

A baby dodo.

I stared at him, and he stared at me. "Mealworm?" I held one out. He gobbled it down and looked for another.

I fed him several before I remembered I hadn't shown him the picture.

I pulled it from the rucksack and held it up.

He didn't seem interested in imprinting. He just wanted more mealworms.

I called him Alan.

I left the dodo picture propped inside the nest. That way, the others would see it right away.

I went to get the others and we watched as the other eleven eggs hatched, one by one. Miss Smallbone was over the moon. "At *last*," she wept. "The Smallbones can hold their heads high again."

"Are they all dodos?" I asked. "Because Dr Gupta wasn't sure they would be."

"Yes," Miss Smallbone said. "Definitely." She squinted at Alan. "Apart from him. He has yellow eyes. Baby dodos are always born with green eyes."

I stroked Alan's head. I didn't mind if he wasn't a dodo. He was still cute. He spent a lot of time trying to scramble over the edge of the nest to get to me.

Jess noticed. "Did you show him the picture?" she whispered.

"No," I whispered back. "I forgot."

"So, you were the first thing he saw?"

I nodded. "I guess."

Jess picked him up and put him in my lap. "There you go, Alan. Say hello to your mum."

FORTY

Miss Smallbone was issuing last-minute instructions. "They stay on mealworms for three days and then move on to the real thing."

Mildred patted a bucket. "We have plenty of those."

Miss Smallbone looked up the beach to a surly-looking Mr Mason. "Keep him busy. I'll leave you the spud gun and the King Edwards, in case he misbehaves."

"What's he doing?" I peered at him.

"We've given him a break from the latrines. He's weaving us sunbeds from mango twigs." Muriel gave him a coquettish wave.

Mildred squinted over. "Mr Mason? She tapped her

watch. "Almost time for our mid-morning cocktail. Coconut and lime today, I think."

It was hard to leave Alan. I thought my heart might break. He peered forlornly after me as I trudged down the beach to *The Red Tornado*. He might not be a dodo, but I'd watched him take his first wobbly steps. I'd fed him his first mealworm.

He thought I was his mum.

I wiped away a tear.

Miss Smallbone was waiting at the wheel. "Where's your sister?" she asked.

"Here." Jess jumped in between me and Boris. "I went back for Dr Gupta's rucksack. I thought she might want it."

Mildred and Muriel came to see us off. Jess shouted goodbye.

I couldn't shout anything. I felt too sad.

Miss Smallbone fired up the engine and pushed down the throttle. She gave her sisters a wave. "Look how happy they are," she said. "Pirates always feel at home on islands."

"It's nice you made up with them," Jess said. "Family's important." She looked at Miss Smallbone. "It's sad you never got the chance to know Martin."

"Martin?" Miss Smallbone shot out through the gap in the rocks. "Oh, I found Martin a few years back."

We stared at her. "I thought he drowned?" I said.

Miss Smallbone shook her head. "They made him walk the plank, but he didn't drown. It turned out there was one thing Martin was brilliant at."

"What?" I asked.

"Swimming," Miss Smallbone said.

"He made it to shore?" Jess asked.

"Washed up in Devon." Miss Smallbone spun the wheel. "Changed his name from Smallbone to Smith so Father couldn't track him down. Still loves the sea. Takes tourists out on a fishing boat."

Jess blinked. "Our great-grandad takes tourists out on a fishing boat," she said. "In Devon."

"*His* name's Martin Smith," I said. "Wouldn't it be funny if—" I stopped and looked at Miss Smallbone.

She raised an eyebrow.

"Miss Smallbone," I said. "Are you our great-aunt?"

FORTY-ONE

Our great-aunt, Mary Smallbone, said she hadn't wanted to tell us we were related until she'd made amends for the crimes of her ancestors.

"*Dodo à l'orange,*" she said. "It wouldn't have been fair, lumbering you with that."

I could hardly believe it. I was descended from *pirates*. Who *cared* what my school report said? I was as far from average as could be.

"There's one more thing." Miss Smallbone headed for the open sea. "I left Hogweed Hall to George, but there was something I wanted *you* to have, Jess. The problem was, I'd mislaid it."

"Oh." Jess was lounging on Boris at the back of the boat, trailing her hand in the water. "Never mind."

"I put it somewhere safe, then couldn't remember where. I left you the thing I loved most in the world instead." Miss Smallbone gave Boris a fond look.

Jess rumpled his fur. "He's OK, I guess."

"I thought he'd be good for you. Give you something to think about, other than race suits."

"I don't think about them *all* the time," Jess said.

Miss Smallbone adjusted the throttle. "I must say this boat is *marvellous*. I'm thinking of a round-the-world trip. I might take this instead of *The Windy Pig*."

I looked at her. "Did you ever find the thing you lost?"

Miss Smallbone nodded. "I did. Just the other day, in fact." She rummaged in the pocket of her britches. "I'd popped it in an egg cup for safekeeping. Here it is." She held something up.

Something that glowed in the sun.

Jess and I stared at it.

"Is that the Constantine Ruby?" I asked.

Miss Smallbone preened. "It is."

"You had it all along?" Jess blinked at it.

"Since I was tiny," Miss Smallbone said. "I found it in a box of napkin rings. I had no idea it was valuable. I gave it away. Beryl Brushface had come for Christmas.

She asked if I had any trinkets to put in the pudding. I let
her have the ruby, along with a sixpence and a thimble."

"And you got it in your helping?" Jess said.

Miss Smallbone shook her head. "Mildred got it in
hers, but she kicked up a fuss because she wanted the
sixpence. Nanny made me swap."

"And you've had it ever since?" I said.

"That's right." Miss Smallbone turned to Jess. "Shall
we exchange, then? You get the ruby, like I planned – and
I'll have Boris back?"

Jess blinked. "You want Boris back?"

"If that's OK?"

Jess looked at Boris snoring in the sun, then at Miss Smallbone. "But I never wear jewellery," she said. "And I really like Boris."

Miss Smallbone beamed. "I *knew* it." She held out the ruby. "You can keep both."

FORTY-TWO

It was great to be back at Hogweed Hall. The first thing Miss Smallbone did was take down the portrait of Sidney "Squid-Hands" Smallbone and put it in the vaults. "The rats might get it," she said. "Let's hope so."

I took a pen to Mildred and Muriel's room and finished off the family tree. I put Martin back where he should be and added Grandad and Mum and Dad, and me and Jess. Then I sat back and admired my ancestors. It was nice to have a big family, even if some of them were blackhearts.

I wondered how Alan was getting along on Hornswagg. I pictured his little yellow eyes and sighed. I hoped he wasn't missing me too much.

Jess barged in, followed by Boris. "There you are."

She held up Dr Gupta's rucksack. "This needs to go back," she said. "Can you take it up?"

I still felt a bit nervous around Dr Gupta. "Can't you do it?"

"I've got the championships this afternoon. I need to get ready."

"OK," I said. I took it.

"Check it's empty first," Jess ordered. "You don't want to give it back full of mouldy mealworms."

I didn't see why *she* couldn't have checked, but I couldn't be bothered to argue. I unbuckled the flap and peered inside.

Something glared up at me.

ALAN!

Oh, Alan.

I scooped him up.

I couldn't speak.

I looked over at Jess.

"What was I supposed to do?" she said. "You're his mum."

My eyes filled with tears.

"Thank you," I said.

FORTY-THREE

Miss Smallbone was in the attic, packing. She didn't seem to mind that Jess had smuggled Alan off the island. "It's not like he's one of the dodos," she said. "A parrot will fit right in at Hogweed Hall."

Apart from the old books on the side, the lab was ever so empty.

Miss Smallbone saw me looking. "Dr Gupta's gone," she said. "She was offered Mr Mason's job at the Natural History Museum. Absolutely *thrilled*, she was."

"Was she pleased all the eggs hatched?" I asked.

"Over the moon," Miss Smallbone said. "Eleven dodos, back where they belong. Her lifetime's work, completed." She snapped the lid shut on her suitcase. "You should both be very proud."

"You too," I said.

Miss Smallbone gave a chortle. "Muriel and Mildred have been in touch. They're enjoying the simple life and would like to stay a little longer."

"Are they still digging?" Jess asked.

"Oh yes." Miss Smallbone nodded.

Jess looked at her. "Will you ever tell them you had the ruby all along?"

"One day." Miss Smallbone sniggered. "I'm *sure* they'll see the funny side."

I wasn't sure they *would*.

"I've decided not to sell it," Jess said. "I can do without a race suit."

"Of course you can." Miss Smallbone picked up her case. "I'm off. I'll send postcards," she said. "Let you know how I'm getting on."

"Where *are* you going?" I asked.

"Back to fetch *The Windy Pig*. And then. . ." Miss Smallbone checked over her shoulder in case someone who shouldn't be was listening. She paused. "Promise you won't tell a soul?"

"I *absolutely* promise." I meant it.

"So do I," Jess said.

"There was a second map," Miss Smallbone whispered.

"A second map?" I blinked.

"It was with the journals. It shows all the places Sidney buried his pirate treasure." Miss Smallbone gave an excited clap. "I've treated myself to a metal detector and a spade."

I stared at her. "Can I come?"

Miss Smallbone gasped and grabbed me by the shoulders. "That would be *wonderful*, George!" she cried. "I'd LOVE to have you along—"

"Ahem." Jess stepped forward. "I think *not*."

She did have a point. Mum was due back, and Jess wouldn't find it easy explaining where I'd gone. Also, I had Alan to think about. He was only young and might feel unsettled if we went off again so soon.

Miss Smallbone was disappointed, but said not to worry and that maybe we could sort something out if Mum went on another work trip? She gave us both a hug.

"I'll be in touch," she said.

She gave Boris a pat, and then she was gone.

I stared after her.

"Hey." Jess was flicking through one of the books.

"What?" I said.

"Back on Hornswagg," she said. "Didn't Miss Smallbone say dodo chicks had *green* eyes?"

"Yes," I said.

"Read that." Jess tapped the first page of *Everything You Need to Know About Dodos*.

I read the bit she was pointing to. "That can't be right," I said. "It says dodo chicks have yellow—"

Alan squawked.

I looked down into his little yellow eyes.

"Oh," I said.

FORTY-FOUR

Mum was thrilled that there were no wildebeest or llamas in the garden on her return. She admired Alan greatly, and said a bird was a fantastic choice of pet. "Is he a parrot?" she asked. "Where did you get him?"

I was about to tell her everything, but Jess stepped on my foot. "We got him from the pet shop," she said. "The big one out of town. And *yes*, he's a parrot."

"He's absolutely gorgeous." Mum offered him a mealworm. "Will he be featuring on your YouTube channel, George?"

I shook my head. "It wouldn't be fair on him. All that attention."

"You've just missed Mildred and Muriel," Jess said. "They were ever so sorry, but they had an appointment."

"I'll text them later and say thank you," Mum said. "Such kind old ladies. They gave me lovely card before I left."

"I know," I said. "I signed it."

Mum gave Jess a hug. "Well done on winning the championship."

"She was *amazing*," I said.

"When *isn't* she." Mum beamed with pride.

"She was the only one in a regular swim suit," I said. "She still won by miles."

"I pretended I was escaping from a shark," Jess said.

"You are funny." Mum said. She picked up a letter from the table and started to open it.

"What's that?" I asked.

Mum looked at the front of the envelope. "It's from the school, I think."

The school?

I blinked.

It was probably about my terrible mock results.

Never mind. "Come on, Alan," I said. "Let's go and dig for worms."

THE END

MISS SMALLBONE'S CHOCOLATE TIFFIN

INGREDIENTS

110G BUTTER

2 TABLESPOONS SUGAR

2 TABLESPOONS GOLDEN SYRUP

4 TEASPOONS COCOA POWDER

225G DIGESTIVE BISCUITS, ROUGHLY CRUSHED

100G OF MALTESERS, LIGHTLY SQUASHED

1 SMALL HANDFUL OF RAISINS

400G CHOCOLATE

~~100G OF GRAVY GRANULES~~

(BLURRRGH, DO NOT PUT THIS IN! - GEORGE)

METHOD

GET A GROWN-UP TO HELP YOU MELT THE
BUTTER, SUGAR, SYRUP AND COCOA TOGETHER
IN A SAUCEPAN. ADD THE CRUSHED BISCUITS.
STIR TO COMBINE, THEN MIX IN THE
MALTESERS AND RAISINS.

LINE AND GREASE A 20CM SQUARE tIN.
POUR tHE MIXtURE IN AND PRESS It DOWN
FIRMLY. ~~tHEN SPRINKLE tHE GRAVY ON tOP.~~

(DEFINITELY LEAVE THIS BIT OUT – GEORGE)

BREAK UP tHE CHOCOLAtE AND PUt tHE BIts
YOU HAVEN'T EATEN INtO A SMALL MIXING
BOWL. CAREFULLY PLACE tHE BOWL WItH tHE
CHOCOLAtE IN It INtO A MUCH BIGGER BOWL
OF HOt (NOt BOILING) WATER. LEAVE FOR
tEN MINUtES tO MELt. StIR SOMEtIMES.
tHEN POUR tHE MELtED CHOCOLAtE OVER tHE
BISCUIt MIXtURE.

PUt tHE tIN INtO tHE FRIDGE AND LEAVE
FOR AN HOUR tO SEt.

GARNISH WItH MARSHMALLOWS AND SERVE.

ACKNOWLEDGEMENTS

I'd like to say a huge thank you to everyone at Scholastic, particularly Linas Alsenas, Peter Matthews, Lauren Fortune and Leanne Burke, who have turned my words into such a beautiful book.

Thank you to my editor, Yasmin Morrissey, for her insight, kindness, and wonderful enthusiasm, to Liam Drane for his stunning design and to Isabelle Follath for her gorgeous illustrations.

In the real world, the thanks go to those who kept me entertained and therefore, sane. Meryl Thomas, Claire & Pete Robins, Lorraine & Rob Hart, Jude & Neil Reynolds, Ali & John Haxworth, Vicky Baker, Carineh Shahbazian, Jo Rogers, Nic Slowey-Hall, Maia Sissons and Katherine Ogilvie. We have a lot of pandemic-friendly catching up to do – until then, keep sending the memes.

Thank you to Beryl, my much-adored mum who

always has a story to tell, and the inspirational Mitch, who was right about so many things.

I'd like to flag my appreciation for Ruth Griffiths's writerly friendship and her ability to spot a plot hole at a hundred paces, Julian of Grove Geeks for his calm and reassuring wizardry in the face of tech disaster, Janine Amos, whose words stayed with me, and the much-missed Sparky Robins, lurcher extraordinaire and sole source of my doggy knowledge.

Then there's my four lovely daughters, Isobel, Eva, Hattie and Daisy, who fill my days with laughter and bring me cups of tea (of varying quality, it has to be said).

And the biggest thank you of all to my agent, the fabulous Kate Shaw, who is never not amazing.

ABOUT THE AUTHOR

Kita Mitchell always dreamt of becoming an author. She wrote and illustrated her first work, *Cindersmella*, at the age of eight. It was swiftly and cruelly rejected by publishers. The sequels, *Mouldilocks and the Three Bears* and *Repunsmell* were equally badly received. Disheartened, she became an animator – but the feeling she should write for children never went away. Many years later, Kita graduated from the Bath Spa MA in Writing for Young People, and her first book, *Grandma Dangerous and the Dog of Destiny*, was published in 2018. She has been writing ever since.

Kita lives in Oxfordshire with four daughters and a hamster.